6

THE HAMMERS OF FINGAL

'NEARLY eleven o'clock it was, with the darkness coming down like a blanket. Suddenly I heard them—the Hammers of Fingal. The sparks from the anvil flew up against the sky, and I knew that someone in Breckadale was needing a coffin.'

Old Peggy has a vivid Celtic imagination; yet Hamish Heathergill, writer of detective stories, is convinced that her account of what she saw is true, in the sense that an impressionist painting is true.

His friend, Inspector Duncan MacLeod, has a more down-to-earth approach to the problem of murder; and in the end it is the policeman's logic which reveals a vicious killer.

ANGUS MacVICAR

The Hammers of Fingal

M

JOHN LONG
London

JOHN LONG LIMITED

178-202 Great Portland Street, London, W.1

AN IMPRINT OF THE HUTCHINSON GROUP

London Melbourne Sydney
Auckland Bombay Toronto
Johannesburg New York

First published 1963

*This book has been set in the Times type face.
It has been printed in Great Britain on Antique
Wove paper by Cheltenham Press Ltd., Cheltenham.*

ANGUS MacVICAR

The Hammers of Fingal

M

JOHN LONG
London

JOHN LONG LIMITED

178-202 Great Portland Street, London, W.1

AN IMPRINT OF THE HUTCHINSON GROUP

London Melbourne Sydney
Auckland Bombay Toronto
Johannesburg New York

★

First published 1963

*This book has been set in the Times type face.
It has been printed in Great Britain on Antique
Wove paper by Cheltenham Press Ltd., Cheltenham.*

To
Olive and Teddy
Exiles from Breckadale

The rushing rattle of wave upon wave
  Comes echoing out like a crackle of guns
As the sea-swell lifts and assaults the cave;
  And the song of the smiths through the hammering runs:
      'Doom will sound ere we are free.
        (Wield them, *gillean*; keep your pledges!)
      Till no motion stirs the sea
        Hissing forges feed the sledges.'

In murky gloom when the storm-king rides,
  The smith and his sons work all night long;
The hammers crash on the anvil sides,
  And loud 'mid the din is the blacksmiths' song:
      'Fingal's armour shape once more.
        (Wield them, *gillean*; keep your pledges!)
      Work is hard when tempests roar;
        Glowing forges feed the sledges.'

The waters are calm and the winds die;
  Slowly the ripples slide o'er the shingle;
In the cave is a patter and murm'ring sigh,
  And the song of the smiths and the wavelets mingle:
      'Ullin's harp-frame weld again.
        (Softly, *gillean*, keep your pledges!)
      Ease your bodies, ease your pain;
        Dim the forge, lay by the sledges.'

1

(1)

Two nights before they found the body, Janet and Hamish Heathergill decided to celebrate the publication of his twenty-ninth detective novel with a drink at the Breckadale Arms. Janet said it was his best story to date. She had said that about them all, out of a warm and generous heart.

As he changed that evening in their bedroom, with the westering sun glinting on the dressing-table mirror, she came in from the sitting-room. 'Hamish, you do take ages putting on a tie! It's nearly half-past eight.'

'Shan't be a second. The hotel's bound to be full of summer visitors. Nothing like a smart Argylls tie for putting you on the "old boy" wavelength.'

'The vanity of men!' Standing on tip-toe to cope with his gangling height, she knotted the tie and smoothed down the wings of his collar.

'Hey, what a smashing frock!' he said, becoming aware of something blue and white and figure-revealing.

9

'D'you think so?'

He kissed her. Into her ear he said, 'If you like we could cancel that drink!'

She rescued herself, laughing and smoothing her frock. 'Even after fifteen years – and with all those grey hairs?'

'H'm. Where's my sports jacket?'

'In the wardrobe. Beside your old flannels.'

As he put it on, a thudding sound floated in through the open window – a heavy, metallic sound, curiously muffled as if it came from underground. She moved close to him again, blue eyes darkling.

'What's the matter?' he said. 'It's only the Hammers of Fingal.'

'I know. But it always frightens me.'

'Nonsense!'

She sat down by the dressing-table and ran a comb through her thick dark hair. 'It's what they say about it, I suppose. Old Peggy's stories.'

'Pure superstition. Any clean handkerchiefs?'

'In the bottom drawer.'

While he rummaged, Hamish said, 'Bruce has written a new poem called *The Hammers of Fingal*.'

'About the cave?'

'Yes. He read it through to me yesterday. Wonderful!'

'He's close enough to his subject.' She began to use lipstick. 'Between his house and the cave there's only Duncraig.'

Finding a handkerchief, he crumpled it into his pocket and sat down on the bed. 'You know, I'd give all the books I've ever published to be able to write just one of Bruce Cattanach's poems.'

'You think he's brilliant, don't you?'

'I know he's brilliant. He has everything, Janet – insight, courage, integrity, an honest ear for words. Sometimes I wish I were his age again.'

She put the lipstick in her bag and smiled across. 'You've done a lot to encourage him, darling. Those introductions. Converting the old lifeboat house into a comfortable home for him. Installing the telephone—'

'It's the least an old hack can do for a thoroughbred.'

She jumped up and tweaked his ear. 'Less of the Celtic twilight! They don't translate old hacks into about twenty different languages. Come on – hold my coat.'

He laughed and obeyed. 'We don't need the car, do we?'

'On a lovely July evening like this I'd much rather walk.'

She had a last look at herself in the mirror, then caught his hand and steered him out through the hall into the sunshine at the front door. Across the placid bay, the Rock of Duncraig glowed greenish-red. The thudding sound had vanished under a quiet sea-hush.

'I expect we'll find Bruce at the hotel before us,' she said. 'Since Sheena McRae started in the cocktail bar he's been a regular customer!'

'I don't blame him. Sheena's the second most beautiful woman in Breckadale.'

He bowed and ushered her through the gate leading on to the main road.

11

Square and white, the Breckadale Arms stood on the hillside half-a-mile above the Heathergills' bungalow. Lazy guests could sit at the window of the cocktail bar and enjoy an airy vista – to their left the Firth of Clyde, with Ailsa Craig and the isle of Sanda interrupting a smoothness of blue water enclosed by the low lands of Ayr and Wigtonshire in the distance; to their right, seventeen miles away across the North Channel, the round blue hills of Antrim looking like the backdrop in a Walt Disney cartoon; and in the immediate foreground, fringed with bent and summer caravans, a yellow beach curving in from the golf course towards the rugged pile of Duncraig, where Bruce Cattanach's house, near the old jetty, sheltered beneath it in quietude.

But that evening, though the cocktail bar was fairly full, nobody was showing much interest in the view.

To the fair-haired girl behind the counter Bruce Cattanach said, 'I'll have another, Sheena.'

'Are you sure? This will be your third in half-an-hour.'

'Half pints won't do me much harm.'

Wearing narrow, navy blue trousers and a grey wind-cheater, he was stocky and broad, with black close-cut hair and the vital pale face of a Pictish-bred Highlander. At twenty-four she was only two years younger; yet despite the sophistication of her hair-style and close fitting sleeveless frock, she looked almost like a child compared with him. This may have been due in part to her fair colouring – and also, perhaps, to a hint of innocence and vulnerability in her eyes.

The background clatter of talk made her lean closer across the counter. 'Can you afford them?' she asked.

'Now look!' His dark head came close to hers. 'I signed the contract yesterday. A weekly book-review for the *Gazette*, ten guineas a time. I'm in the money!'

With anxious affection she shook her head. 'You'll never be in the money, Bruce. You don't know the first thing about money!'

'If you're trying to tell me I ought to go in for big business, like – like that glistening pair over there—'

'Oh, all right.' She caught and tamed his gesturing thumb and took his glass to refill it. 'You're so stubborn! But make this one last out – please!'

As she worked the beer-handle, he emitted an actor's sigh and addressed the ceiling. 'Who would have thought it! Her face, fair-haloed, warm and kind – her form sweet symphony of grace; her heart of flinty stone!'

She smiled, extracting his change from the cash-register. 'You made that up on the spur of the moment, didn't you?'

'How d'you know?'

For a moment they lost contact with their surroundings – the brittle talk, the smoke, the chromium-bright counter, the bottles and mirrors behind it. A quick, tense tenderness made them unaware of anything except themselves.

Sheena said quietly, 'Because my heart isn't nearly hard enough, as far as you're concerned.'

'I wish that were true.' He wasn't acting any more.

13

'I wish – ' Abruptly he broke off and raised his glass. 'Oh, well, here's to life and love!' He took a mouthful, then added, lowering his voice, 'What about tonight?'

She shook her head, unwillingly. 'I must go straight home. I'm sorry, Bruce.'

'Oh, hell!'

'Don't you remember – on a Friday evening – the doctor comes in to see Father?'

'So he does. What a selfish clot I am!'

'You're neither selfish nor a clot.' She touched his hand. 'I shan't be in a hurry tomorrow night, if – if it suits you.'

'If it suits me!' He was suddenly as happy and eager as a boy. 'I'll be counting the minutes! Sixty multiplied by twenty-four – what's that? I'm no good at arithmetic, but it's a hell of a lot of minutes!'

She caught her breath and whispered, 'For me, too.'

'D'you mean that? . . .'

Out of the corner of her eye she saw the door of the bar swing open. The moment passed, and she stood up straight. 'Bruce – Mr. and Mrs. Heathergill have just come in.'

'Eh?'

'They want to speak to you, I think.'

He focussed on reality. 'Oh, right.' He smiled and took up his glass. 'I'll be back soon,' he told her.

(3)

She watched him join the author and his wife, glad that he should be in their company.

14

She liked the Heathergills and found it difficult to realize that in terms of age they could have been her parents. Trim, capable and small, Janet might have passed for thirty-five. As for Hamish, his hair was greying and his face lined from long hours wrestling with words; but he retained the tall angularity of adolescence, and his absent-minded enthusiasms were unexpected in a man of nearly fifty.

Sheena always admired the way Janet humoured him, with the gentle confidence of love. Sometimes, allowing herself to dream of a miracle still unaccomplished, she wondered if after fifteen years she and Bruce could be so happy together. Janet had been at a university. She herself had gone no further than the fifth grade in grammar school. Was this important?

What did a writer who spent hours each day in loneliness and pain of spirit require from a wife? She would be able to comfort Bruce's body – that she knew; but could she solace his mind? How had Janet done it for Hamish? Some day she must take courage and ask her advice – though she suspected that her own problem might be more difficult. Bruce felt things more deeply than Hamish. He had a grimmer sense of purpose – a more uncompromising belief in right and wrong. . . .

'Hi, there, sweetheart! Same again, please.'

She started out of her thoughts like a sleeper roused by an alarm. 'Er – of course, Mr. McDermott. Three doubles?'

'Yes. On the rocks.' He was good-looking in a blond, well-nourished way – 'glistening' as Bruce had put it;

15

his sports jacket and flannels, like his accent, had the style of the city. 'Have a spot of something yourself?' he added, eyeing her figure as she broke ice into the glasses.

'No, thank you,' she said.

'Oh, come on! We're celebrating. Reunion with Colin, my country cousin.'

'What's this, Finlay – taking my name in vain?' Colin Campbell lounged in towards the counter, tall and broad, his shock of yellow hair gleaming. 'Hullo, Sheena!' he grinned. 'Long time no see.'

She smiled and nodded. Though he lived in Kinloch she knew Colin fairly well because his work on the telephone lines often brought him to Breckadale. He looked younger and fresher and much less sophisticated than did his cousin.

'Look, Finlay,' he went on, 'I just came to tell you – I don't want a double. Honestly—'

'Be your age, man! I'm paying for it. Scared it'll put you off your golf tomorrow night?'

'There's that.' Colin chuckled as he sprawled loosely against the counter, his big golfer's hands caressing a glass that still held whisky. 'But the main thing is, I can't afford to splash money around like you and Peter. Not at the moment, anyway.'

'Still playing the horses?'

'Well . . . '

'All right – we'll make it singles next time. But your prospects are better than you think, old boy.'

'How come?'

Sheena reached for a full bottle of Black and White and fitted a measure to its neck. The two cousins had dropped their voices, but she couldn't help overhearing.

'In confidence – when Alice and I finally separated last year, I changed my will.'

Colin's golf-tanned forehead wrinkled. 'I still don't get it.'

'Currently you are – what do they call it? – my residual legatee. Some day you could be a rich man, saying "Nuts" to the Post Office and to all those bookies you keep in business.'

It was a casual observation, made to cover an awkward moment in the party. This was plain to Sheena. But Colin reacted with uncharacteristic seriousness.

'I – I never expected that, Finlay.'

'Well, you're my only relative, after all.' McDermott laughed it off and turned. 'Oh, the drinks, sweetheart! Sorry, I have nothing but a fiver.' As she did arithmetic on the cash-register, he handed two of the glasses to his cousin. 'Keep what I've told you under your hat,' he said. 'And take this one across to Peter.'

'Right.' Colin recaptured his grin and waved burdened hands to Sheena. 'Be seeing you,' he called to her.

She counted out McDermott's change, thinking how alike the two men were, despite the obvious difference in their social backgrounds. The eyes were the same, vividly blue and containing a hint of assured recklessness. The chins were the same, squarely purposeful in contrast with full-lipped mouths. And their fair colouring stemmed from a common Nordic root.

'Sure you won't have something?' he asked.

'No, thank you. I scarcely drink at all.'

'Too bad.' He sampled his Black and White, then smiled at her with admiration. 'You know, sweetheart, my partner and I only booked in here today – that's him, Peter Marlin, with the bald head and calculating eye, talking to Colin – but I'm sure of one thing already. I'm going to enjoy this holiday.'

Though now aware of the kind of man he was, she still sensed his attraction. 'Breckadale is beautiful in summer,' she said, putting up a barrier of primness.

'I know. Who'd think that smoky old Kinloch is only ten miles away!'

'Do you play golf, like your cousin?'

'A bit. Not so expertly as Colin, though.'

'Well, he's our local champion.'

'So it seems. He's challenged Peter and me to a match tomorrow night – playing our better ball. For a fiver, no less!'

'On the Breckadale course?'

'M'm.' He drank more of his whisky. 'He's driving down from Kinloch in his own car and meeting us at the clubhouse at seven. Which reminds me, we'll have to order high tea tomorrow instead of dinner.'

'I didn't know until now that Colin *had* a cousin.'

'We were brought up together in Kinloch,' he told her, fanning the spark of intimacy. 'By my grandmother. I beat it to Glasgow as soon as I could and founded my electrical goods firm. McDermott and Marlin – you must have heard of it?'

18

'Oh, yes! I have one of your electric irons.'

He smiled, fleshy lips parting over white teeth. 'Any complaints?'

'None at all,' she answered, laughing.

'There you are – another satisfied customer. Peter and I work like niggers to satisfy you, too. But Colin – well, he's different. He seems quite happy to spend his life as an ordinary Post Office engineer. In Kinloch, of all places!'

She lifted her shoulders. 'He stays in a very nice little private hotel. He has his golf, his car—'

'Don't tell me *you* approve of the small town mentality!'

'What do you mean?'

'Well – a fine-looking girl like yourself. Ever since I spotted you behind the bar I've had a feeling we could get on together.'

The innocence drained from her face. 'Didn't I hear you say you were married?'

'A case of marry in haste and repent.' He sighed. 'Alice and I haven't lived together for years. Not as man and wife. But she won't stand for a divorce – on religious grounds.'

'I see.'

'But never mind my troubles,' he said gallantly. 'Let's talk about you. Do you live here, in the hotel?'

She was uneasy. The sun was going down outside, spoiling the colour of the sea. The talk in the bar was growing louder, the atmosphere warmer. Through a haze of spirit-scented cigarette smoke she looked across

19

to where Bruce was chatting with the Heathergills, knowing that he hated her being pawed about – even mentally – by flashy guests like Finlay McDermott. She caught his eye and his grim half-smile at once betrayed the fact that he had been watching. She felt suddenly lonely and wished it was closing time.

To McDermott she said, 'I keep house for my father in the village. He's been an invalid for years. He used to be a fisherman, but one night two skiffs collided in a fog and he injured his back. In summer I take this job to help out.'

'Ever go dancing in Kinloch?'

'Sometimes.'

The tip of his tongue slid round his lower lip. He was about to say something when a resonant bass voice rose above the general babble, 'I say – come here, Finlay!'

She spoke quickly. 'Excuse me, it's Mr. Marlin.'

'Oh, blast!'

'Colin's calling you, too.'

McDermott glanced behind him and the youthfulness slid from his face. 'What country clod-hoppers have they got in tow with now! Right, just coming!' he called, adding confidentially, 'Be seeing you, Sheena.'

He moved off, and she sighed a little with relief. But then she saw that his friends were introducing him to the Heathergills and Bruce. Her uneasiness returned.

(4)

Over in the curve of the big bay window Janet was smiling up at McDermott. 'I'm sure you're going to love

20

Breckadale. We're your neighbours – the little bungalow down there by the shore.'

'I see.'

'Mr. Marlin has already promised to drop in for coffee one morning.'

'I took up the offer at once,' said Marlin, his dark somewhat inscrutable face creasing into a smile.

'You would, Peter!' But as he turned again to Janet, the momentary sharpness in McDermott's voice was submerged in practised charm. 'My partner,' he said, 'can never resist a pretty lady.'

Though vaguely conscious of irritants beneath the chatter, Hamish shook hands and tried, as was his habit in social exchanges, to emphasise the bright side. 'Nice to see new faces. They look after you pretty well up here in the Breckadale Arms, but my wife does make excellent coffee.'

'I'm sure of it.'

'Finlay,' Marlin put in. 'I don't think you've met Mr. Bruce Cattanach.'

'Mr. Cattanach? Didn't I see you at the bar a minute ago?'

'Very likely,' said Bruce, glowering.

That gusty waves of dislike had suddenly reared up between the two men was obvious to Colin Campbell. He thrust a hand through his thick fair hair and tried the effect of an oil-slick on troubled waters.

'We – er – we installed Mr. Cattanach's telephone only last week. Damned annoyed I was at the time – we had to run the wires in front of the seventeeth green,

21

between it and the burn. They come down to about ten feet at one part. I thought they'd be bound to spoil the shot across the water.'

'Too bad!' sympathised Hamish.

And Janet added, 'Especially as you'd get no sympathy from Bruce. Having been a shinty blue at Glasgow University, he looks down his nose on all golfers! Don't you, Bruce?'

'As it turns out, though,' Colin hurried on, 'the wires don't make all that difference – provided you shoot for the back of the green.'

Marlin's bald head glistened in the warmth of the bar, but his voice was cool enough. 'I can see we're going to have our work cut out, Finlay – tomorrow night, I mean – against a dedicated golfer like this!'

'Don't worry.' McDermott's smile didn't touch his eyes. 'We'll find his Achilles heel. Every golfer has one – like shinty-players, it seems.'

There was another small stab of silence, broken this time by Janet. 'Of course!' she exclaimed, sounding brittle and bright. 'At the moment Bruce's tender spot is that he has to live alone – in what used to be a lifeboat house.' She pointed out through the window. 'You can see it from here – across the bay, right opposite our bungalow. Under Duncraig.'

Pleased with his thrust, McDermott became sociable again. 'Formidable looking,' he declared. 'Duncraig Rock, I mean. Especially now, shadowed in the sunset. Must be a hundred feet high if it's an inch.'

With a dim sense of relief, Hamish said, 'I could tell

you a dozen stories about it. For instance, sixteenth-century wreckers used to put a light on it – a lure for ships.'

He was about to expand this theme, when Bruce interrupted. 'Wreckers don't use lights nowadays. Mostly money. And it's not ships they're after.'

His dour look was for McDermott, who came back sharply, 'I beg your pardon?'

But Marlin laughed, patting his partner's shoulder. 'I don't think you realize we're in a den of lions, Finlay. Literary lions.'

Supporting him, Janet said, 'But they seldom roar like lions – believe me! More like doves. Hamish – do be hospitable and order some drinks.'

Her husband, now fully aware that the conversation had gone awry, hastened to take his cue and create a diversion. 'Yes, yes, of course. Whisky, Marlin?'

'Well – thanks.'

'Just a small one for me, please,' said McDermott without warmth, while Colin smiled and shook his head, indicating his still untouched glass.

'Bruce, what about you?'

'Leave me out, Hamish. But I'll go across and give Sheena the order and help her bring the drinks.'

'Good. Thanks.'

'Your usual, Janet?'

'Please, Bruce. Gin and orange. Mostly orange.'

He thrust a way towards the counter, lively aggression in the set of his shoulders.

With a superior smile, McDermott glanced after him.

'Extraordinary chap! Not what you'd call a "hail-fellow-well met"!'

'I've been trying to tell you,' Marlin said. 'He's Bruce Cattanach, the poet.'

'So what? I've never heard of him.'

At last Hamish was truly shocked. 'Never heard of Bruce Cattanach! He's our new white hope in Scotland. A modern Dunbar.'

'I'm afraid I'm a Philistine,' replied McDermott, with a Philistine's pride in the confession. 'And my wife and Peter here never allow me to forget it.' Then he put the matter aside as of no consequence and turned to Janet. 'Mrs. Heathergill, d'you mind if I open the window?'

'Not at all.'

He went across and raised one of the lower sashes. 'It's got a bit stuffy in here,' he said, returning.

The others nodded. The sound of the sea came faintly, and a small mild wind, carrying the scent of newly-mown grass on the lawns of the hotel, flurried the cigarette smoke.

Betraying no sign of embarrassment at the coupling of his name with that of his partner's wife, Marlin said pleasantly, 'If you haven't read Bruce Cattanach, Finlay, I know you've read Hamish Heathergill.'

'Eh?' For the first time McDermott showed interest. 'Don't tell me this is Hamish Heathergill who writes the detective stories?'

'Dead on target!' grinned Colin.

24

'Pity me,' laughed Janet, 'exposed to every kind of dreadful death!'

'Well, I'm damned!' McDermott's smiling exclamation lightened the whole atmosphere. 'I have a paperback of yours up in my room!'

Hamish made modest noises. 'I make a living out of it, but I don't count myself a writer like Bruce. He's in a different class altogether.'

'Oh, come off it!' McDermott was clearly impressed by the amount of hard cash represented by twenty-nine successful books. 'I must say it's astonishing to find someone like you holed up in a place like Breckadale! Why didn't you tell me, Colin?'

'I never thought.' Smiling in Hamish's direction, Colin added something that he knew would please him. 'In this part of the world we look on Mr. Heathergill as one of ourselves.'

(5)

Sheena and Bruce approached, carrying the drinks.

Full of universal goodwill again, Hamish handed them round, chatting as he did so with Sheena. 'Are you taking Bruce on as a permanent assistant?'

She made a wry face. 'Would it be safe for the tumblers, Mr. Heathergill?'

He laughed and put a pound note on the tray, telling her to keep the change. 'How is your father?'

'Not too bad at all. He's always better when the days get warmer—'

'Hullo, sweetheart!' McDermott had detached himself

25

from the others and come close behind her, face flushed, eyes coveting her body. 'You know, Heathergill,' he said. 'Breckadale has given me two very pleasant surprises. You – and my sweetheart here.' He put an arm about her and kissed her cheek.

She moved quickly aside, colour flooding her face. Bruce moved quickly, too.

Taut with anger, he confronted McDermott. 'Keep your paws off her! She's not your sweetheart!'

The bar quietened. Visitors not in the group by the window looked away and tried to appear as if they weren't listening.

'What's the matter with you?' inquired McDermott, with hard insolence.

'I've warned you – she's not for sale!'

Sheena caught his arm. 'It's all right, Bruce. He didn't mean anything—'

'I know what he means! I know his kind – thinks he's God Almighty because he can splash money about!'

Janet glanced at her husband, but found no comfort in his look of helpless dismay. Marlin remained in the background, curiously intent.

Colin put in, 'Mr. Cattanach, Finlay's not really like that . . .'

'Isn't he, now?'

'Look, Cattanach' – McDermott had drunk a lot of whisky, and his accent was coarsening – 'leave my money out of it and stick to your dreary little poems! Time you grew up!'

Bruce raised his fist. 'By God, I've a good mind to—'

'No, Bruce – please!' Sheena wrapped her arms about him. Half-sobbing, she said, 'I'm sorry, Mr. McDermott, I—'

'Why the hell should *you* be sorry? He'll apologise now – pronto.'

Janet called out, 'Wait!'

The figures in the group were frozen in tableau.

Hamish mumbled, 'Janet, what's up?'

'There it is again,' she said.

In the bitter silence the sound came clear and loud, thudding through their heads.

'Odd,' said Marlin. 'I heard it tonight already. Like the sea hammering against rocks.'

'That's exactly what it is,' replied Hamish, snatching at an opportunity to restore calm. 'The tide running into a cave on the other side of Duncraig – beyond Bruce's house. It has a Gaelic name – *Uamh nan Ord* – which means "the cave of the hammers".'

Colin said quickly, 'Isn't there some kind of legend about it?'

'Yes. Fingal's blacksmith and his two sons broke the law of the great Cuchullain. They were banished from Ireland and imprisoned here, in the cave.'

'There's a similar story,' said Janet, imperceptibly relaxing, 'about Mendelssohn's Cave in Staffa.'

His voice still passionate, Bruce rapped out, 'But this one has a tail-piece, McDermott. They say that when you hear the hammers it means a death in Breckadale!'

2

Saturday, 6.55 p.m. to 11 p.m.

(1)

THE following evening, wearing a light nylon golf-jacket and with a cigarette hanging at one side of his mouth, McDermott was in his bedroom, checking the contents of his golf-bag. The door was ajar. A hot July sun made an opaque dazzle of the open window, concealing the distant dark mountains of the Mull of Kintyre which it framed.

Footsteps in the corridor preceded the appearance of Peter Marlin's burly sweatered figure at the door. 'I thought so – still in your bedroom, Finlay. Haven't you got your clubs ready yet?'

'Plenty of time, old boy.'

A flick of irritation showed on the other's face. 'We promised to meet Colin at the clubhouse at seven. It's five to now, and the porter says it'll take us ten minutes to walk there.'

'So what?'

'Maybe we ought to take the car?'

'That would mean dismantling our trollies to load them in the boot.' McDermott flung the stub of his cigarette out of the window and transferred a tartan cover from a discarded brassie to the head of a Number 4 wood. 'No, we'll walk. If we're late it may put him off.'

'Your cousin doesn't seem the nervous type.'

'That's what you think!' said McDermott, taking a handful of peg tees from a pouch in his bag and putting them in his jacket pocket. 'As a matter of fact, he reminds me of my dear wife. Cool and calm on the surface, but – well, when you know how to go about it, Alice and Colin are the two most easily rattled people I know.'

A small pulse beat at one corner of Marlin's mouth. 'During the past few years Alice has had every reason to get rattled.'

His partner smiled. 'That's right, Peter – you stick up for her! But she's not your wife, remember. Not yet.'

'Look here, Finlay—'

'Take it easy, old boy! You're becoming as touchy as that fool Cattanach! I don't mind you being friendly with Alice. On the contrary.' Gaily he lifted the bag and shouldered it, enjoying his power to hurt his partner without fear of retaliation. 'Well, I'm all set. What about another quick one before we go?'

In the corridor, containing himself with habitual patience, Marlin said, 'Finlay, you're here to play golf – not to seduce a barmaid!'

'Ah, but what a barmaid!'

'You'd be well advised to lay off her. I didn't like the look in Cattanach's eye last night.'

They went downstairs and into the front hall, which at the moment was empty, most of the other guests having gone in to dinner.

'That makes it all the more interesting,' said McDermott, fixing his bag on the trolley. 'Still,' he admitted, 'there's a time and a place for everything, I suppose. Got that famous niblick of yours?'

'The 9-iron? I certainly have.' Relieved that once again his partner's spiteful mood was passing, Marlin took his lightweight cap from the hall-stand and permitted himself a small, tight smile. 'Without it I'd feel naked on a golf course!'

'Then we'll tan the hide off him!' The charm was burgeoning again. 'That club's a winner. Come on. Do we take the short cut past Heathergill's bungalow?'

'Yes.' Marlin manoeuvred his trolley out through the open door. 'Then across the main road on to the course.'

'Good.'

'We ought to finish just after ten – before it gets too dark.'

(2)

Just after ten the gloaming was falling on Breckadale. A motionless shadow amongst the rocks, Bruce stood on the shoulder of Duncraig some fifty yards above his house.

Beyond the caravans on the bent he could see tiny coloured figures hurrying along the last few fairways of

30

the golf course, intent upon finishing their rounds before it became too dark to follow the flight of the ball. A lingering heat was causing haze to drift up from the Con as it flowed and rippled past the seventeenth green. He could see cars grouped around the distant clubhouse where lights were already burning. Behind the clubhouse he could just make out the lop-sided shape of the village – solidly stone-built at its eastern end, County Council tiles and bricks giving its western flank a flimsier, gaudier aspect. But the light had become so dull that the inland woods and farms were hidden. In a minute or two the village also would merge with the dusk; then the clubhouse, then the caravans, and finally the beach and his own house immediately below.

There was no wind, but the still air carried many sounds. Children shouted as they played late near the lighted caravans. Gulls complained in crannies on the shore. Someone shouted 'Fore!' on the golf course, raising a skirl of feminine laughter. But the main sound in Bruce's consciousness was the steady beat of the Hammers of Fingal. Sometimes the sea-swells caused by strong Atlantic winds came running in against the shores of Breckadale with startling power, though the winds themselves had died away or taken a different course. This was happening now, and, if anything, the sound of the hammers was growing in volume.

Bruce turned and looked towards the far side of the bay, where lights were blossoming in the hotel. As yet there was no sign of Sheena, and in a moment it would be too dark to see her coming.

31

He scrambled down, slipping and sliding on the rock-strewn turf, and reached the smoother strand. He was eagerly excited at the thought of meeting Sheena; yet his mood had fear and tension in it, too, as if something ugly hovered in the falling night – something ugly in the midst of beauty, like the harsh smell of rotting seaweed which tonight vitiated the clean scents of sea and turf and wild thyme.

He saw a light flick on in the Heathergills' bungalow and wished he could talk about his unease with Hamish and Janet. They always made him feel happier and more able to cope with the hard discipline of living. Hamish's unselfish enthusiasm for his poetry inspired a confidence in his own ability that helped him through lonely spells of work. Janet's sensible concern for his shirts and socks and grocery bills made him feel as if he mattered as a man.

Their plain, ordinary love for each other, continuing unaffected by domestic arguments and irritations, was also a source of pleasure to him. With his casual attitude to household timings, his incredible optimism in the face of awkward truth, his vague helplessness in a crisis, Hamish was clearly a difficult man to live with. But Janet did so in a calm and practical way, chiding him without rancour for cigarette-sprinkled carpets, irregular appearances at meals, late hours of reading, writing and talking. Bruce knew the reason for her patience. Hamish had never become 'a sophisticated adult'. He still treated his wife as if she were twenty and he only a few years older. He still made love to her as he had done on their honeymoon. He still admitted needing her in every way, and this, because she was a woman, made her content.

They had no children. It was a circumstance which must often have saddened them, but they kept their sadness to themselves.

Bruce's brogues crunched in the shingle. The Heathergills took no part in the modern cult of hate and self-indulgence. Could he – a product of modernity – make Sheena happy, as Hamish had made Janet happy? In some respects he knew he was like Hamish – careless of material convention but with a Calvinistic respect for proven spiritual standards; at times floating away from ordinary life on a cloud of wordy excitement but coming back to it in the end with the capacity for love and tenderness unimpaired. Nevertheless, there was in him a temper which perhaps Hamish had escaped – a violence geared to sexual desire which he did his best to master and conceal but which might vent itself on the very person he loved the most. He looked truth full in the face and disliked what he saw.

It was now almost completely dark. He stopped in an angle of the shore, close to the bank of bent which was their usual meeting-place.

The beat of the hammers still went on. Was it the old superstition about an imminent death that made him so edgy? There was enough of the Celt in him to make it possible, even though his mind, trained in logic at Glasgow University, contemptuously rejected the idea. Or was it an unusual warmth in the atmosphere which disturbed him – an electric quality which he had often experienced before in the quietness of a summer night?

Words to describe his feelings began to flutter in his brain, words which strangely resolved themselves into a description of Sheena. Dread of something unknown, pulsing excitement at the thought of holding her body in his arms, irritation at the ceaseless thudding in Fingal's Cave – emotions surged in him, back and forth like the nearby waves.

Then suddenly he heard light footsteps on the shingle, and his uneasiness was stifled by the quick pounding of his heart.

'That you, Sheena?'

She stopped for a second, then ran to him, her white dust-coat opening like the wings of a moth. 'Oh, Bruce! I didn't see you, there against the bank. I'm sorry if I'm late.'

He caught her and kissed her, and for a time they clung to each other, trembling.

At last he said, 'I didn't mind waiting. I was making a poem about you.'

She leant back, smiling, her hair spread brightly against his taut left arm. 'You weren't! Not about me?'

'I was.' She was so small, so apparently fragile that a rush of tenderness made it difficult for him to keep his voice steady. 'Shakespeare wrote sonnets to his dark lady. Why shouldn't I write them to my fair one? Anyway,' he went on, doing his best to recapture common sense, 'you said some time after ten, and it's not half-past yet.'

34

She pulled his head down and kissed his bristly dark cheek. 'I had to wash up after the bar closed,' she explained. 'And you know how particular the manager is about the glasses.'

'I know.' His love for her surged in him, constricting his throat. His arm tightened. 'Sheena, won't you come in – into my house, I mean? I'll put the kettle on. We'll have a cup of tea together.'

In his mind was a dream of ordinary domestic happiness such as the Heathergills enjoyed; but he saw the clouding in her eyes and knew that for the time being at any rate it must remain a dream.

'Not now, Bruce,' she answered, quietly. 'Not yet. If I did, and people got to know about it—'

'To hell with people!'

If she was disturbed by his reaction she didn't show it. She stretched up and gently smoothed his forehead. 'Darling, you can never say to hell with people. You can't afford to. If not for their sake, then for the sake of your own happiness.'

Her small persuasive smile kindled another in him. 'Maybe you're right,' he admitted. 'You usually are, come to think of it. In that case I'll see you home across the golf course.'

She knew he was disappointed and tried to make amends. 'There's no hurry,' she said, tucking her head close against his shoulder. 'Not tonight. It's so lovely and warm – and the sea, so friendly.'

'I'm glad. Sheena, I need you!'

She looked up at him, her eyes misting in the

half-light. 'I need you, too,' she whispered and reached up and kissed him with sudden passion.

After a moment they sat down together on the bank. The beat of Fingal's hammers was becoming louder, but they didn't notice. Not then.

'I love you,' he said, holding her close. 'More than anything else in this world. Why won't you say you'll marry me?'

'It's my father, Bruce.'

'But I told you – he could live with us.'

There was a pause. A small wind eddied about them.

She looked away and plucked at a stem of bent by her feet. 'Not only that, darling. I'm just a – just a girl from the village. You've been to the University. Some day you'll be famous, and—'

'What has that got to do with it?'

'I – I must be sure.'

'Sure of what?' Anxiety made his voice softer and lighter, almost like a boy's. 'Don't you love me?'

'I love you, Bruce.'

'Then what are you worrying about?'

'I must be sure that you love me.'

He acted quickly, turning her head round so that she faced him again. 'Sheena, I'm crazy about you—'

'No, wait!' Her body resisted him. 'I must be sure that you're not thinking about me as – as an ideal. A kind of living pin-up girl.'

'The things you say!' Relief made him laugh as he kissed her. 'No wonder I love you!'

'But I'm serious.' She wanted to have done with

practical arguments, to drown them in a flood of love; but contrariness, born of a kind of inferiority complex, drove her on. 'It's one thing being romantic – here in the dark, listening to the sea, listening to the sound from the cave, kissing each other.' Her eyes pled for understanding. 'It's different being married.'

He smiled and gently lifted her chin with his fist. 'You'd make any man a wonderful wife. Even a prince or a king. You're good, you're sweet, you're innocent—'

She put a hand over his mouth. 'Bruce, it's so easy for you to say these things. You're a writer. You can put words together. You can put glamour into anything.'

'Now, look—'

'Let me finish, dear.'

'Why should I let you finish?' His voice hardened. 'I resent you saying that. As if – as if I could say these things to anybody.'

'I'm sorry.' She found happiness slipping away, but could do nothing to curb her contrariness of spirit. 'Please try to see it from my point of view. I love you to tell me I could be a princess or a queen – what girl wouldn't. But – but I never know if you're in earnest. I mean – you were so angry last night with Mr. McDermott, and—'

'I had every right to be!'

'No, Bruce. You say I'm good and sweet and innocent, but the way you acted – well, why can't you trust me to speak to men like him? If you loved me you'd trust me. You wouldn't make a fuss.'

'So I was making a fuss?'

With one part of his brain he knew he was being childish. Though lovers' quarrels were outmoded in cool modern society, he was in the midst of one, like the soppiest character dreamt up by Ethel M. Dell. But he couldn't help it. As had happened last night in the bar, a primitive instinct was riding him.

She felt the arm about her beginning to shake. She loved him and longed to make him happy.

But she answered, 'Yes. I was ashamed.'

He stood up, shoes slithering in soft sand. 'God! Now we're getting at the truth!'

She scrambled to her feet, shocked by the savageness in his eyes. 'Darling!' she exclaimed, catching the lapels of his jacket. 'I know you were trying to protect me, but—'

'You *liked* being pawed about by McDermott!'

'I didn't. I hated it. But I can take care of myself.'

'Could be. But I'll tell you this – I'm not going to stand aside like a damned stookie and let you carry on with every rich Casanova who comes into that hotel!'

She drew in her breath. 'I don't "carry on", as you call it! I wasn't "carrying on"!'

'How do I know you haven't been talking to him all evening – up there in the bar?'

She made a gesture of appeasement. 'He's been out all night – golfing with Mr. Marlin and Colin Campbell. When I left the hotel just now he and Mr. Marlin hadn't come back.'

'Did you talk to him before he went out?'

'You have no right to ask me that!' Her face was

38

white in the luminous dark, her voice unsteady. 'But – well, I did talk to him. Just for a minute or two, after his meal. He had a drink before he went upstairs to get his clubs.'

'You seem to be well informed about Mr. McDermott.'

'There you are!' The making of her point hurt her so much that she began to cry. 'It would be the same if we were married. You'd never trust me.'

Her tears jerked him back to some kind of sanity. 'But I do trust you. I love you!'

He caught her hands, but she pushed him away and began to climb the bank. 'I wish you did, Bruce. I – I'm going home.'

He struggled after her through the sand. 'But Sheena . . .'

'It's no good.' She knuckled her eyes like a lost child. 'Not tonight, anyway. Something has come between us. And that noise is getting on my nerves! Going on and on and on—'

'Darling, listen to me!' He put his arm about her shoulders. 'Look, I'll confess. I'm not only a selfish clot, I'm a jealous clot.'

She stopped and faced him. 'I'm going, by myself,' she said. 'It's not far to the village.'

'Let me come with you.'

'I told you, it's no good. We'd just go on quarrelling. It's that sort of night. Still and tense and – and ready to explode.'

There was nothing to be seen from where they stood

near the top of the bank, though the golf course was only a few yards away. He felt sick and dreary.

'Very well,' he answered, lifting her hand and kissing it.

The gesture was so unexpected and his eyes were so sad that she began to cry again. For a second she wavered. Then – 'Good night, Bruce,' she said quickly and turned and hurried away.

He watched her white coat disappear in the dark. For a time he stood there silent until at last the beat of the hammers burst a tight knot in his head and he muttered to himself, 'Oh, hell! Glamour, did she say?'

(3)

At about ten minutes to eleven Peter Marlin wheeled two trollies into the front hall of the hotel – his own and McDermott's – and parked them in a corner. At the moment he didn't trouble to unfix the bags of clubs. He was hot and tired, for it had been a stiff climb up from the main road; and as he took off his cap and hung it on the stand, his thoughts were on a drink. He badly needed one.

Hearing the talk and laughter of other guests in the lounge, he decided to wait in the deserted hall. He slumped down in a wheezy basket-chair and was about to ring a bell on the glass-topped table beside it when the porter, having heard the front door open and shut, emerged from a dark opening marked *Staff – Private* beyond the telephone boxes.

'Oh, there you are!' Marlin greeted him. 'Not too late for a drink, eh?'

'Och, not at all, sir. Not for a guest like yourself.'

By his tongue the man was obviously a native of Breckadale. He wore corduroy trousers and a battle-dress top dyed navy blue. His age might have been anything from forty to fifty, and there was a humorous but wary friendliness about his thin brown face that was typical of Kintyre. His name, in fact, was Patrick Reid McConnachie, which probably summed up a mixed ancestry with roots in Ireland, Ayrshire and Argyll.

'Right,' said Marlin. 'I'll have it here in the hall—'

The phone in one of the boxes began to ring. With a murmured apology, McConnachie went to answer it.

'It's for you, sir,' he said, coming back. 'Mr. Campbell – him you were golfing with.'

'Oh, thanks.' Marlin got up.

'Quite a coincidence, the phone going the very moment you arrive.'

'Yes, indeed. Get me a double Scotch, will you? On the rocks.'

'Okay, sir. I'll be back by the time you've finished.'

Vaguely surprised that young Campbell should be using the telephone when by rights he ought to have been travelling between Breckadale and Kinloch, Marlin entered the box and picked up the receiver.

'Yes, Colin?'

'Oh, Peter. I'm speaking from a call-box just outside Kinloch.'

'I see.' That was one mystery solved.

Colin's voice went on, quick and urgent like his golf,

'Driving back in the car, it suddenly occured to me I'd forgotten to return your 9-iron. I borrowed it at the fifteenth, remember, for that left-hand shot out of the whins.'

Marlin experienced a curious sense of relief. 'Oh, yes. I'd forgotten, too,' he said.

'So I stopped at the nearest call-box to apologize. I'll bring it down tomorrow, Sunday, when I'm off duty.'

'Good of you to ring, old boy.' Colin's keen and vigorous approach to the game of golf showed him to possess a share of family ruthlessness; but there was in him a warmth that Finlay lacked, and Marlin was inclined to like his partner's cousin. He added, 'I'm sorry you hadn't time after the match to come up here for a drink.'

'I wanted to explain about that, too.'

'As a matter of fact,' Marlin said, 'I'm still on my own. When Finlay left us at the clubhouse to go and look for that ball he shanked into the burn, I expected him back in a few minutes. But he hasn't shown up yet.'

'Maybe it wasn't the ball he went to find.'

'That did occur to me. Especially when he insisted on going alone and asked me to take his trolley.'

'Sheena McRae, d'you think?'

'Could be. I understand she goes home across the golf course.'

Colin sighed into the distant mouthpiece. 'Well,' he said, 'I guess that's Finlay's business.'

'Sure.'

The young engineer hesitated for a second, then continued quickly, 'I hope you didn't think I was a bit off-hand at the clubhouse just now – I mean, refusing your invitation to have a drink with you at the hotel there?'

'Off-hand? By no means.'

'The plain fact is, I was skint – after forking out that fiver to you and Finlay.'

'Good Lord, that shouldn't have stopped you!'

'I like to stand my hand. Poor but independent – that's me.' For a moment Colin sounded like his slick and citified cousin. 'However, it was a good game,' he went on. 'I didn't expect to get beaten, I may tell you – but I enjoyed it.'

'We were lucky. That putt I sank on the last green was a stinker.'

'Left-handers have always been my downfall.' Colin's laugh came over the wire without real humour. Almost bitterly he added, 'You pulled Finlay through all right.'

'I often have to,' Marlin told him. 'Not only on the golf course.'

'Well, it's late,' said Colin, sighing again. 'Nearly eleven. So I shan't keep you. Be seeing you tomorrow.'

'Splendid.'

'I'll bring the 9-iron. Good night, Peter.'

'Good night, Colin. Thanks a lot.'

In the hall McConnachie was waiting with his drink. 'Scotch on the rocks, sir.'

'Well done. Put it on my bill.' He sat down in the basket-chair and drank gratefully.

The porter lingered. 'Do you hear them, sir?' he asked, his eyes on the dark oblong of open window.

'The Hammers of Fingal, you mean?'

'Ay. They're going strong tonight.'

Marlin shivered and took another gulp of whisky. He said, 'You don't believe in that old superstition, do you?'

'Well, for myself, I was brought up an unbeliever, as it were.' The man gave a slow, crooked smile. 'But, och, there are plenty of folk hereabouts – like old Peggy McAllister – who treat it as gospel.'

'So I'm told.'

'Though, mind you, some of them have also seen two moons in the sky – after a night in the bar!'

Marlin laughed.

'But it's a strange thing,' McConnachie went on, his mobile face becoming serious again. 'The last two times we heard the hammers, somebody did die. An old *bodach* up the glen and a baby with croup. And when two deaths take place in Breckadale – well, nearly always there's a third.'

For a moment Marlin stared at him. Then he drained his glass and growled, 'Huh! Highland hokum!'

'Like another, sir?'

'Not just now. I think I'll have a turn outside.' He heaved himself out of the basket-chair. 'I may meet Mr. McDermott on his way up the hill.'

'Okay.'

'In any case I'll be back in a few minutes. Will you still be here?'

'Och, ay – until after twelve o'clock.'

'Fine. I'll probably need another drink then.'

As he picked up his cap from the stand and went towards the front door, McConnachie called after him, 'There's no hurry, sir. No hurry at all.'

Outside in the meagrely-lit courtyard, Marlin found that a chill night wind was blowing. But the beat of the hammers had begun to fade.

3

(1)

'MUSHROOMS to right of us, mushrooms to left of us!' muttered Hamish, dropping another handful into Janet's basket. 'Don't you think that's just about plenty?'

'One or two more, darling. In case we fancy some tomorrow.'

They went on gathering.

The day was so young and fresh that the sun, emerging from a bank of innocuous cloud behind Sanda, had still to dry off the dew. It sparkled along the seventeenth fairway like spilt quicksilver.

Except for themselves, the golf course was deserted. In the hotel and in the caravans wise visitors were still in bed. But a distant barking came from farmyard collies bringing in cows for the milking, and smoke had begun to float up from a few of the village chimneys. A quarter of a mile to their left lay the mouth of the Con, hemmed in by rocks which had spilled down from Duncraig. Its tidal waters were on the ebb; the sea

46

beyond was quiet, and there was no hammering in Fingal's Cave under the Rock. Indeed, the only sounds came from seabirds wheeling and screaming on the edge of the burn about a hundred yards inland.

Hamish was slightly disgruntled, because he wasn't used to getting up so early. 'What a performance!' he said, discovering a promising clutch of fat, pink-lined mushrooms and bending down to pick them. 'Hauling me out of bed at seven o'clock on a Sunday morning for this kind of caper!'

'If we hadn't been early those people in the caravans would have bagged them all.' As fresh as the day in a white blouse and Black Watch tartan jeans, Janet was unmoved by his plight. 'Anyway,' she pointed out, 'think how you're going to enjoy your bacon and eggs and mushrooms when we get back!'

'It was *you* who wanted mushrooms – not me!' As he came towards her and topped up the basket an idea occurred to him. 'Come to think of it,' he exclaimed, with mock excitement, 'you said you had a sudden craving. Don't tell me – don't tell me you're hiding anything?'

'Really, Hamish!' she laughed. 'Wait until I start asking for the coal-bucket before you get ideas!' She lifted up the basket and squeezed his arm. 'But that should be enough. You've been very sweet and patient and understanding. Let's take the short cut home across the burn – by the Golfers' Bridge.'

He chuckled. 'Right. For this relief much thanks.'

They walked through the silver dew, leaving behind the dark trail of their footprints. As they approached

47

the bridge – an erection of flimsy, tarred wood which gave easier access to the seventeenth green than the main bridge a hundred yards downstream – the gulls and red-shanked sand-pipers were still cackling noisily above the margin of the burn.

Looking across at the green's emerald smoothness, with the limp red flag marking the hole and two telephone lines sagging down to ten feet above one corner, Hamish said, 'Those are the wires Colin Campbell was talking about on Friday night. They do seem a bit in the way.'

Janet nodded. 'Poor Colin! He may be nuts about golf and horses, but I prefer him to that cousin of his, Mr. Don Juan McDermott.'

'Bruce would agree with you there!'

'Oh – and Bruce! What gets into him? He'll lose Sheena McRae altogether if he doesn't watch out. And serve him right!'

'It's the way he's made.' Not for the first time, Hamish came stoutly to the defence of his protégé. 'He *feels* everything so much more than an ordinary person. That's why he's a poet.'

'Then I'm glad you're not a poet,' she returned flatly.

He tried reasoning with her. 'He's violently in love at the moment and quite naturally inclined to be unstable. But he'll settle down, you'll see. He could make Sheena very happy.'

'I suppose so. I'm very fond of Bruce, really. She'd be good for him, too. She has character, that girl.'

They climbed on to the bridge.

48

As her sandals rattled two loose boards, he caught her arm. 'Watch it, Janet! It seems to get narrower and shakier every time we cross it.'

'Old fuss-pot!' she gave him back. 'I'm not nearly as decrepit as you think!'

Suddenly, half-way across, she stopped, her free hand clutching the wooden rail. 'Hamish!' she whispered.

He followed the direction of her eyes. Under the canopy of squabbling birds something was lying in the shallows of the burn, on the opposite bank from the green. At first it looked to him like a log of light-coloured wood. Then a sluggish movement of the water revealed a face and lank fair hair.

'My God, it's a man!' he said. 'Lying on his back.'

He retraced his steps on the bridge and ran towards the patch of sandy shingle. Putting down her basket, Janet followed.

The birds screamed and flapped away, then flew back and settled on the seventeenth fairway to watch from a distance.

Hamish knelt down.

'Has there been an accident?' she panted, hurrying down the bank.

'Don't come too close!' he warned her, but his voice broke as he gulped back nausea.

'Darling, I'm not a child.'

Then she saw whose body it was and stood stiff and straight, her hands to her temples. 'His head, Hamish! The left side of his head! Something struck him.'

49

He rose awkwardly to his feet and tried unsuccessfully to be sick. She went to him at once, supporting his head like a mother with a child.

After a time he eased himself upright.

She said, 'He's dead, isn't he?'

'Yes. Yes, he's dead.' This was a situation similar to many he had described in his books; but reality was a daunting experience.

'What are we going to do?'

He groped for a cigarette and lit it. His brain came to terms with the sodden flannels, the bloodstained golf-jacket, the red pulpy ruin of the head, and his sickness passed. He made a sober effort to think.

'Look,' he said finally. 'I must get a doctor – and the police.' Phrases used by his fictional characters now came automatically, helping to steady him and shape a plan of action. 'I'll phone from Bruce's place – it's just beyond the sand-dunes there. You – you'd better go home.'

'Could I ring his partner at the hotel – Mr. Marlin?'

'Yes, do that, Janet. Tell him to come here at once. He can get in touch with Colin Campbell later.'

'All right. Oh, Hamish – take care!'

Why she said it, neither of them could understand; but in any event, this was no time to consider submerged motives. They hurried across the rickety bridge – where, with a look almost of surprise, Janet found and picked up her basket of mushrooms – and parted on the eighteenth tee, she to skirt the caravan park on her way home, he to cross the dunes towards Duncraig.

Sheltered on its right hand by the dunes, and behind and on its left by the Rock itself, the old lifeboat house had been erected some ninety years before – a narrow, slate-roofed building with space for the lifeboat on the ground floor and living quarters for the caretaker in the storey above. Immediately before the first German War, when motor-vessels were displacing the old pulling and sailing craft, the Breckadale lifeboat had become redundant, its functions being taken over by a powerful boat stationed in Kinloch. In consequence the house had become semi-derelict, used only by wandering tinker families and occasional homeless tramps.

In the eighteenth century the stone jetty in front had been a busy, bustling terminus for passenger and cargo traffic with Antrim across the channel; and it was said that Burke and Hare, the body snatchers, had landed there en route for the graveyards of Edinburgh. Nowadays it served only a handful of local fishermen and the boat which ran weekly with passengers and mail to the isle of Sanda. Its rings and bollards were crumbling with rust, and the gulls used it as a communal latrine.

But the lifeboat house had been given a face-lift.

Three years before, while at Broadcasting House in Glasgow to see the radio version of one of his books being recorded as a Light Programme serial, Hamish had encountered Bruce Cattanach, who since his graduation, had been working with the BBC as an assistant producer. In spite of an age difference of more than twenty years, the two men had taken a quick interest in each other. Bruce had warmed to the lack of literary 'side' in a writer who had achieved material success. For his part, Hamish had been excited to meet a young poet whose promising talent he had already discovered in the *Gazette*.

Finding that Bruce was single with no near relatives living, Hamish had suggested that he ought to leave his constricting job and become a full-time writer. The clinch-point of the argument had been his purchase and transformation into a comfortable home of the old lifeboat house, which he said Bruce could have at a nominal rent. In the end, Bruce had accepted the offer with sincere but darkly inarticulate gratitude, and though as yet only two-thirds of his first novel was written, he had been able to live well enough on the proceeds of poems, articles and reviews in the *Gazette* and some of the English weeklies. On the whole, the arrangement had been a success, and Hamish – even more than Bruce – looked forward to the publication of a novel which he passionately hoped would establish a bright new reputation.

As a good tenant, Bruce had improved the ground outside the house. The old cement tracks on which the lifeboat bogie had travelled to and from the water had been picked away and replaced by a garden containing flowers and vegetables, with a narrow gravel path running through it up to the front door. It was along this path that Hamish now went running, his thoughts utterly divorced from literary subjects.

He tried to thrust open the narrow, yellow front door.

Finding it locked, he began to hammer on it with his fists.

'Bruce! Are you awake, Bruce!'

The sun was still hidden behind Duncraig, and the house was in shadow, but the scents of sea-washed tangle trapped by the jetty and of the cat-mint frothing at the path edge were keen in the warming air. He was unaware of them.

As he hammered, the door opened. Jaws black and unshaven, wearing faded blue jeans and a fisherman's high-collared blue guernsey, Bruce stared at him.

'What the hell's gone wrong?'

Hamish leant against the door-jamb, breathing hard. 'I – I didn't expect you'd be up,' he answered, with stupid inconsequence.

'I couldn't sleep. There was a poem in my head. But look—'

Hamish pulled himself together. 'There's been an accident,' he said.

'What?'

'McDermott. Opposite the seventeenth green over there. He's lying in the sand, half in and half out of the water, with his head smashed in.'

'My God!' Bruce's vague and uncertain expression blazed into horror. 'Is he dead?'

'Yes. May I use your phone?'

'Of course. Come in, Hamish. I'm sorry I wasn't quite with you at first.'

He led the way through the plaster-board hallway into the big living-room.

On a table in the middle of the floor note-books,

copy paper and pens crowded round a portable type-writer. A mug containing dregs of cold tea sat on top of a Roget's *Thesaurus*. Cases spilling over with books ran round three walls. In the other wall a deep, old fashioned fireplace had been fitted with a coal stove and an electric cooker. Crossed above the wooden mantle-piece were two shinty-sticks. The windows were tightly closed, and a cluster of electric bulbs, still burning palely in the ceiling, was mocked by daylight.

On a magazine-littered desk near the door stood the telephone. Hamish jerked off the receiver and dialled a number.

Leaning against the table, Bruce said, 'The – the police, eh?'

'Inspector Duncan MacLeod in Kinloch. As you know, he and I are old friends. He'll bring a doctor.'

'What a hell of a thing!'

Hamish nodded, dimly concerned about his friend's dishevelled appearance and the stale untidiness of the room. Then his attention was caught by a voice in the receiver.

'Kinloch Police. Bar officer here.'

'This is Hamish Heathergill. Could I speak to Inspector MacLeod, please?'

'I'm sorry, sir. He's not due in before the afternoon.'

'Put me through to his home, will you?'

'At this time on a Sunday morning?'

'It's urgent! I must speak to him at once.'

'Well, sir – if it's like that. . . . Will you hold on a minute, please?'

'Yes, I'll hold on.'

Bruce had stirred himself out of physical lethargy, switching off the light and opening a window. Now he put water into an electric kettle which he plugged in and placed on top of the cooker.

'How did you find him?' he asked, clearing one end of the table and arranging the articles of his trade more neatly at the other. 'McDermott, I mean.'

'Janet and I were gathering mushrooms on the seventeenth fairway. She's gone home. She'll let Marlin know.'

From a cupboard beside the fireplace Bruce took two cups, a bowl of sugar and a small jug of milk and laid them on the table. Then, from the caddy on the mantelpiece, he put three spoonfuls of tea into a teapot and waited for the kettle to come to the boil. He was thinking, 'God! What will Sheena say?'

Hamish put a hand over the mouthpiece of the receiver. 'Once I get through to MacLeod, will you – will you come with me?'

'What?'

'The body must be guarded till the police arrive.'

'Oh, yes. Yes, I'll come, Hamish. But first we'll have a cup of tea. And maybe a biscuit. It's a bad thing dealing with death on an empty stomach.'

As the kettle came to the boil, a slightly cool Hebridean voice crackled in the telephone. 'MacLeod here. What on earth has come over you, Hamish? At this hour of the day—'

'I'm sorry, Duncan. But my wife and I – we have just found the body of a man.'

The Inspector's coolness vanished.

3

Sporting a brown Harris-tweed jacket and a Donegal hat with a pheasant's feather in it, MacLeod lumbered up the bank, solid and square as an Olympic shot-putter. 'Well, Hamish,' he said, 'that's just about it.'

The body lay in its original position on the damp sand. But now, beside it, the police doctor was fastening his bag, and Sergeant MacPherson was taking a used film out of his camera. Two medical orderlies were emerging with a stretcher from an ambulance which stood alongside the police car on the opposite bank.

The time was nearly half-past eight.

'What do you think?' said Hamish, doing his best to conceal the fact that during the past hour the horror in his mind had been transmuted into excited curiosity. 'Is it a case of . . .'

'Sergeant MacPherson will be taking another batch of pictures when he changes the film,' replied MacLeod, ponderously oblique. 'But Dr. Kennedy says he's through – for the time being at any rate. I expect you and Mr. Cattanach will want to be going home now.'

Though he badly needed his breakfast, Hamish felt inclined to resist the suggestion. It was the first time he had participated in a serious police investigation, and he found himself disliking the thought of being pushed out into the cold at such an early stage. Bruce, however, had a different view.

'I'll be glad to get away,' he said. 'You know, Inspector,

it's all wrong. The scent of the damp grass, the sunlight on the burn, the quietness – and that – that dead thing.'

MacLeod's darkly-browed grey eyes betrayed no reaction. 'It was good of you both to help,' he replied, in an official monotone.

'By the way,' said Hamish, like a small boy about to ask a favour of his teacher, 'could you tell me – er – please don't think I'm being inquisitive, Duncan . . .'

'Go on.'

'The doctor. I mean – can he tell when McDermott was killed?'

'There's no secret about that. Some time between half-past ten and eleven o'clock last night.'

'I see. But—'

'Last night?' interrupted Bruce, frowning.

MacLeod's official attitude slipped a little. Sharply he said, 'Does anything strike you, Mr. Cattanach?'

'No, I was just thinking. People might have passed by in the dark – quite near – without knowing.'

A thistledown of speculation hung in the air, but it was blown aside at once by a burst of talk from Hamish. A brilliant idea had occurred to him.

'Duncan, you're far from home here in Breckadale. If you'd care to use my bungalow – for interviews, interrogation, that kind of thing. I mean, you'd have a lot more privacy than in the hotel.'

'Thanks, Hamish.' MacLeod smiled. 'I may take you up on that.'

'Oh, good! My wife will be – er . . . ' He was going to

57

say 'delighted', but an unexpected spasm of conscience intervened. 'Janet knows how to look after people,' he compromised.

Some yards distant, on a strip of turf on the bank, lay a green waterproof cloth on which was spread a variety of articles. Bruce had walked across to look at them.

Now he said, 'Inspector – what are these?'

With Hamish in attendance, MacLeod joined him. 'Didn't you notice? We took them from the dead man's pockets.' He knelt down to indicate each item. 'A golf-ball – a 7 Dunlop – practically new. It fell out of his hand when the doctor moved him. A silver cigarette-case. A lighter. Plastic tees. A white silk handkerchief. Seven single pound notes. And – oh, yes – this photo, this snapshot.' He took the slightly torn and crumpled print and, rising without haste, held it up for inspection. 'A very nice-looking girl. I was going to ask if either of you knew her.'

Hamish drew in his breath. Wearing a bikini, Sheena stood on the rocks at the edge of a sea-pool, arms outstretched as if preparing to dive. Her hair was hidden beneath a bathing cap. She was smiling with obvious happiness at whoever had taken the photograph.

MacLeod said, 'Then you do recognize her?'

It was Bruce who answered. 'Her name is Sheena McRae. She works in the cocktail bar at the Breckadale Arms. I may as well tell you, Inspector – I hope to marry her one day.'

The ambulance men, assisted by Dr. Kennedy and Sergeant MacPherson, were easing the stiff corpse on to the stretcher. A gull hovered above them and flapped away, mewing sadly. Hamish found that the palms of his hands were sweating.

With unaltered expression MacLeod loomed above Bruce. 'Any idea why McDermott should have been in possession of this photo?'

'None at all.'

'No? Well, it may not be important.'

As the loose boards in the bridge gave a double rattle they looked up to see Peter Marlin coming quickly towards them. He had on the flannels and grey sweater in which he had played golf the night before, but his head was bare.

'Look, Heathergill, your wife told me I was wanted here. But that was all.' Though he had shaved, the skin on his cheeks was colourless and dry.

Hamish introduced him to the inspector.

MacLeod said, 'I am afraid I have bad news for you, sir – about your partner.'

'Finlay? His bed hasn't been slept in. I went out to meet him last night, but—'

His attention was caught by movement in the stretcher-party. Quickly he strode across, brown brogues crunching in the shingle. He lifted a corner of the sheet and saw the dead face, with its bruising and lacerations.

He turned again to MacLeod. 'My God!' he said, and his washed-out, heavy-lidded eyes were unusually bright. 'It's murder!'

'Ay, Mr. Marlin. It's murder.'

4

(1)

MELLOWED by distance, the bell of the village church began to ring for the service at eleven-thirty. Hamish heard it and had a momentary feeling of regret that for once he and Janet would be absent from their gallery pew.

A few minutes later he entered the kitchen, trying hard not to overdo an ingratiating smile. 'Hullo, Janet – how goes it?'

'See for yourself!'

Pots were steaming on the electric cooker. She moved one to the side and returned to the peeling of potatoes at the sink. He couldn't help feeling that her welcome was coolish.

'You suit that apron,' he persevered. 'It's the colour, I suppose. You always look marvellous in anything red.'

She plopped another peeled potato into the waiting pot. 'Thank you,' she said.

He moved closer and put an arm about her waist. 'Look, Janet – could you possibly do a spot of lunch for the inspector? Nothing elaborate – just a snack . . .'

She smacked down the knife and faced him, hands on hips. 'I knew it!' she exclaimed.

'Eh? Knew what?'

'Hamish, you make a living out of murder. I don't mind that, so long as it's only fiction. But why on earth do you want to get mixed up in the real thing?' Her voice rose. 'Why on earth do you want to fill this house with enormous policemen?'

He flapped distressful hands. 'Ssh, not so loud! He may hear you!'

'Oh, nonsense!'

'Duncan's a friend of mine,' he pointed out. 'He keeps me right on police procedure in my books. And anyway, Janet, it's our duty as citizens to do all we can to help and—'

'All right, all right!' She gave it up and put the pot of potatoes on the cooker. 'If only you'd use your eyes, you'd see that I have anticipated your wishes – that I *am* cooking a meal for your precious inspector! Nothing elaborate, as you say, but still – more than a snack.'

He smiled with real pleasure. 'I might have known!' he said, kissing the nape of her neck. 'Janet, you're marvellous—'

'Spare me the flannel! It's a wonder you don't invite him to sleep here as well!'

'Good heavens, I'd never put you to all that trouble! No, no – he'll sleep at the Breckadale Arms. But he has a number of people to question, and if we can give him lunch and tea—'

'Tea as well?'

'Yes, Janet. I mean, think how awkward it would be if he had to go rushing off for every meal. I mean, he'll get the job done far more quickly if we let him have a bite of something between interviews. I mean—'

'What you mean, darling, is that it's going to be most exciting for *you*. Suspicion with lunch – revelation for tea.'

'Well, you know how it is. My job. The fashion in novels nowadays is a semi-documentary background. This is just the kind of experience I need. Of course, if you'd been the usual sort of incompetent, nagging wife, I'd never have dreamt of inviting him to the house. But you're so calm, so capable, such a splendid hostess. Duncan himself has often said so.'

'How nice of him!'

'Oh, come off it, Janet – it's not like you to be sarcastic!'

To his relief, she finally put aside her martyrdom and began to laugh.

After a time, sprinkling salt into the potato-pot she said, 'Who's in the study with him now?'

'Peter Marlin.'

Her forehead puckered. 'There's a strange sort of man for you!'

'H'm. Quite the gentleman, though – to outward appearances.'

'That's just it. Maybe it's a result of his business training – I'm not sure – but I have the impression of a gauze curtain hiding what he really is.'

62

'Well—'

'That sallow face and balding head, and the kind of hood he brings down over his eyes – oh, I don't know. Anyway, Inspector MacLeod will get very little out of him, or I'm mistaken.'

'I wish I could be there to hear Duncan putting the questions.'

'Well, you can't. So you'd better just go along to the shop and fetch the milk and the Sunday papers. By the time you get back lunch ought to be ready.'

'Right, Janet. Would you like me to buy you a box of chocolates?'

'To sweeten me up? Go on – get out of my hair!'

(2)

Having been invited to occupy a low chair which faced the sunny window, Marlin had an obvious excuse for bringing the hood down over his eyes; but on the other side of Hamish's desk – clean and tidy for once – the inspector sat with his back to the light and wondered, like Janet, if the habit might have a psychological as well as a physical significance.

'Smoke if you like,' he said.

'No, thank you.'

'Ah, well. . . . Now – this game of golf you had.' At fifty, MacLeod still played in police competitions off a handicap of six and, when his timing was right, could hit the ball prodigious distances. 'When was it arranged?'

'On Friday evening, in the Breckadale Arms. Colin Campbell to play our better ball. We had a fiver on the result.'

'Who suggested it – the match, I mean?'

'It came out that Colin is local champion. I said that even a champion might find it difficult to beat the better ball of two fairly competent golfers. For a while we argued about this, then Colin challenged us.'

'Surely five pounds was a hefty stake for a Post Office engineer?'

'Finlay insisted on what he called "a reasonable bet". And Colin appears to be quite a gambler.'

'H'm. Now tell me, Mr. Marlin – the match finished at the last hole. You and McDermott won?'

'Yes. I sank a four-yard putt.'

'Nerves of steel, eh?'

A waif of a smile wandered into Marlin's unyielding expression. 'As one of our Walker Cup men once put it, I was "trembling with bravery".'

MacLeod smiled, too. As a golfer he warmed to this human touch. As a policeman he said, 'What was the time then?'

'I'm not certain. Coming on for half-past ten, probably. We changed our shoes in the clubhouse and talked and smoked for a minute or two. When we came out it was almost dark.'

'What happened afterwards?'

'Finlay said he was going back to the burn at the seventeenth to see if he could fish out the ball he'd lost. A shank with a 7-iron.'

'Stiffening up on the shot across the water to the green?'

'Very likely. Colin and I both offered to go with him, but he didn't seem to want that, so I suggested to Colin that he and I should have a drink up at the hotel.'

'That didn't come off either?'

'Colin said he'd prefer to go straight home to Kinloch. I walked to the hotel, taking Finlay's trolley and my own.'

'According to McConnachie, the porter, you arrived there at ten to eleven?'

'That's right.'

MacLeod nodded. 'A ten-minute walk – it seems to fit in. And at about nine minutes to eleven you had a phone call from Campbell?'

'Yes. From a call-box, two miles from Kinloch.'

'About eleven minutes to cover eight miles. Ay, just about right.' MacLeod heaved his huge bulk forward against the desk. Having scribbled a note on his pad, he looked up and said, 'One small point, Mr. Marlin. You received this call. You had a drink. The porter says you went out again for a few minutes.'

'Twenty to be exact.'

The window was open. MacLeod heard the front gate creak and looked round to see Hamish gangling up the short driveway with a load of milk and papers. A glance at his wrist-watch showed it to be twelve forty-five – almost lunch-time.

He faced Marlin again. 'You didn't take the car?'

'I walked, expecting to meet Finlay on the way.'

'But, of course, you didn't?'

'No. I came back, had another drink and then turned in. I was tired – after the golf.'

'Ay.' The inspector settled back in the swivel-chair, tapping strong front teeth with his pen-butt. 'Oh, by the way – McDermott's widow,' he said, as if the matter were inconsequential. 'You told me you'd be getting in touch with her in Glasgow?'

'I phoned her, an hour ago.' Marlin's face seemed suddenly paler, more strained. 'She's coming for the funeral on Tuesday. Both she and Colin think he ought to be buried in the family lair in Kinloch.'

'Poor woman!' The words were sympathetic, but the voice had a timbre of calculation. 'This must have been a sad shock for her?'

'A shock, Inspector. But not a sad one.'

'Like that, eh?'

'Like that, I'm afraid.'

'H'm. Yourself now. You'll be staying at the Breckadale Arms, I take it – until Tuesday?'

'Yes.' Again a small smile flickered across Marlin's face. 'I shan't try to make a run for it.'

'Why should you?'

'Why, indeed!'

MacLeod rose, with the effect of a tank emerging from a wood. 'Well, that's about all – for the moment. Any loose ends will be tied up by Colin Campbell – I'm pretty sure of that. He's coming here to see me this afternoon.'

'I know. He was coming in any case to return my

9-iron, so I've invited him to lunch with me at the hotel first.' Marlin also stood up, flexing his shoulders as if to remove stiffness. 'By the way,' he added, 'do you – do you suspect anyone?'

'I suspect everybody. That's my unenviable job.'

'Yes, yes – of course. If I can do anything else to help . . .'

'I'll let you know, Mr. Marlin. I'll let you know. Good afternoon.'

(3)

At lunch Hamish was hospitable, bravely concealing his disappointment that interesting disclosures by Duncan were absent from the agenda.

He was inclined to be annoyed with Janet, too. Every time he referred to the murder she seemed to take a perverse satisfaction in reopening with Duncan what seemed to him to be a completely arid discussion on the subject of interior grates. But he subdued his annoyance, persuading himself that the afternoon would almost certainly be different. Indeed, by the time he had taken his Sunday afternoon walk and read all the book reviews in the *Sunday Times* and the *Observer*, it was conceivable that an arrest might have been made.

An arrest? In theoretical terms murder was interesting – even exciting in a way, but in practice . . .

The others were talking about under-floor draughts and back-to-back heating. It sounded normal and un-dramatic; but as he swallowed a final cube of Dunlop cheese, he found himself becoming curiously cold and tense.

Metaphorically he shook himself.

. . . Don't start getting ideas, Heathergill. The trouble is you've written far too many books with tortuous psychological backgrounds. Approach the problem from an ordinary, common-sense point of view and the fact becomes obvious that nobody you know could possibly be a murderer. Surely you have enough knowledge of the human character to be certain of that! A tramp, maybe. Even a drunken visitor from one of the caravans. There's your answer – a stranger, an out-sider. . . .

Feeling happier as a result of this smart essay in self-deception, he smiled and said, 'Cigarette, Duncan?'

'No, thanks. I'll have one with Campbell when he comes. By the way, Mrs. Heathergill – have you heard of the Clereflame?'

'I've seen it advertised.'

'My missus was in Glasgow last month and saw one at the Ideal Homes Exhibition in the Kelvin Hall. Very economical, she says.'

They were off again. Hamish sighed and took a sip of coffee. But even the flavour of Janet's celebrated brew was today a trifle disappointing.

At about two o'clock, however, this less than animated conversation was interrupted by the arrival of Colin Campbell. Colin did his best to appear normally bright and courteous; but to Hamish, who ushered him into the study, it was evident that outward show camouflaged considerable emotion. Blond, tanned and big-boned, he smiled quickly and spoke with drawling calm; but the smile failed to conceal the anxiety in his eyes, and the slow voice had a ragged edge to it. And, after all, as Hamish told himself, wasn't it natural that the violent death of a cousin should cause him distress? The murder had been disturbing for everyone concerned. How much more intimately it must affect the victim's next-of-kin.

Hamish didn't often help Janet with the washing-up after lunch, but today he did, in an effort to appease his conscience. During the operation, however, their talk proved to be intermittent and disjointed. In Hamish's case, the reason was simple. Excited curiosity was now giving place to a sober knowledge that the situation, in essence, was drab and ugly, and that somewhere near at hand there lurked a murderer. Accustomed to his moods and, after fifteen years, better able to appreciate his mental processes than he was himself, Janet knew what he was thinking and refrained, therefore, from asking questions which might make him even gloomier and more anxious.

When the last plate had been racked, he suggested that they might go for a walk together. But she pointed out that one of them would have to stay behind to deal with possible phone calls and visitors for the inspector.

'You go, darling. I'll be perfectly happy in the sitting-room with the papers.'

This made him feel guiltier than ever, but he had become so restless and uneasy that he made no attempt to argue. 'All right. I'll not be long,' he promised, taking his stick with the polished sheep's horn crook from the hall-stand.

Urgently he made his way across the dunes to the seventeenth green, where he found Sergeant Mac-Pherson directing a mixed squad of three policemen, half-a-dozen local youths and about a score of caravanners in a systematic search of the burn and its immediate surroundings. This was what he had expected to find, for Duncan had told him that having spent the morning in routine questioning of people in the village and in the caravans, his men would be engaged during the afternoon in trying to locate the weapon that had killed McDermott.

Amongst the crowd he looked in vain for Bruce. He had an impulse to go and visit the lifeboat house, but he resisted it. A nagging fear of what Bruce might decide to tell him – if he were at home – made resistance easier.

Some of the visitors who knew him and had read his books made abortive efforts to get from him what they imagined would be an expert opinion on a thrilling mystery. Two teen-age girls with brief shorts, badge-covered jackets and long, lank hair came running to ask for his autograph. He smiled bleakly and signed their books without comment. Inwardly he had a feeling of sick disgust at them and at himself. In ordinary circumstances he enjoyed having females make a fuss of him – especially young ones with long and shapely legs. But now, in this arena of cruel death, long and shapely legs seemed to him vulgarly out of place.

70

He crossed the Golfers' Bridge and came upon Sergeant MacPherson, dark and sharp-featured, prodding thick grass on the bank with a piece of stick.

'Any luck, Sergeant?'

'Not yet, sir.'

Hamish summoned up courage and said, 'No clues from your inquiries this morning?'

'I wouldn't know, sir. All I do is report.' To indicate that the snub was impersonal, the Sergeant smiled and added, 'But I'm sure you've gathered from Inspector MacLeod that this wasn't what you might call a casual murder. I mean, all that stuff in his pockets. Nothing was stolen from McDermott.'

'Except his life,' said Hamish unhappily.

'As you say, sir.'

'Can I help at all?'

MacPherson shook his head. 'We're just about finished. In any case – though we have to check thoroughly, of course – I don't believe we'll find anything.'

As he walked back through the bent, Hamish saw the stooped figure of old Peggy McAllister trudging along the shore in the direction of Bruce's house. The afternoon was warm, with only a slight sea-breeze drifting in from the south-west, but her black woollen shawl was gathered close about her shoulders.

(4)

In the study Colin Campbell lit another cigarette. He said, 'And then, Inspector, Marlin asked me to

71

have a drink with him at the hotel. But losing the game had left me stoney – only half-a-crown in my pocket – so I decided to beat it.'

MacLeod made a note. 'Can you pin-point the time?'

Colin nodded. 'I remember looking at the dashboard clock when I got in the car.' As he tapped his cigarette on the edge of the ash-tray on the desk, it looked tiny in his big, muscular hand. 'It was between twenty-five and twenty to eleven.'

'Good. That tallies. And you stopped at the call-box at approximately ten to?'

'That's right.'

MacLeod glanced across at the young engineer. Though he had seen him often in the streets of Kinloch and on the golf course, he had not actually spoken to him before. He had always liked his healthy, fresh appearance and, with a tinge of regret for his own lost youth, admired his style and power as a golfer; and now, as the interview went on, he mentally compared his frankness of manner with Marlin's caginess.

'Now, Mr. Campbell, when you drove off from the clubhouse, Marlin had already begun to walk back to the hotel?'

'Yes – and Finlay had gone to look for a ball he'd shanked into the burn at the seventeenth. A practically new Dunlop.'

The inspector paused. Then – 'Seems he did find it,' he said.

'How d'you mean?' Colin looked startled.

'When the doctor moved his body it dropped from his hand.'

For the first time the façade of normality cracked a little. 'God, poor Finlay! I thought the whole thing was an excuse to go and meet a girl.'

'He's a married man,' MacLeod reminded him.

'I know.' Colin took a deep breath. 'But separated from his wife. He'd taken a notion of the barmaid at the hotel – Sheena McRae.'

'Ah, Sheena McRae. Who lives in the village, eh?'

'Yes. After the cocktail bar closes at night she often takes a short-cut home through the golf course.'

'Her photograph was found in your cousin's pocket.'

'So – so Marlin has just told me.'

There was a short silence.

Eventually the inspector said, 'Did you know that Bruce Cattanach intends to marry her?'

'I – er – well, yes, I gathered that. He and Finlay had a barney about her in the hotel – two nights ago.'

'Quite.' MacLeod dropped the word into another pool of silence and let the ripples spread.

In his early morning questioning of Hamish and Bruce Cattanach at the scene of the murder he had already discovered a good deal about what had taken place in the cocktail bar on Friday evening. The brittle atmosphere that had existed there – and Hamish's rambling talk about the Hammers of Fingal – would have to be investigated further, if only because they provided a background to McDermott's character and to his relationship with various friends and acquaintances. In the meantime the inspector had become aware of a nebulous light in a long, dark tunnel. His instinct was to allow it to grow naturally, without creating any strong draughts that might kill it.

'Quite,' he repeated, and waited.

Colin crushed out his cigarette. 'Look, Inspector – Finlay may have been a bit of a lad. If it comes to that, none of us is a saint. But he was the only relative I had. Tell me, how did he die? Who killed him?'

If MacLeod was disappointed by this reaction he didn't show it. 'I can tell you *how* he died,' he said, heavily. 'Darkness was coming down, but he spotted the ball and waded into the burn to retrieve it. Then someone – someone surprised him. He was thrown on his back – by a simple trip and push most likely – and as he lay there on the verge, half-stunned, the murderer straddled his body and swung repeatedly at the left side of his head with some kind of club. We found blurred footprints in the sand and shingle. Unidentifiable, of course.'

'A club, Inspector?'

'A golf-club, a long-handled hammer, a shinty-stick. Even an ordinary walking-stick with a heavy crook.'

'I see. God, what a thing to happen to poor Finlay!'

(5)

While MacLeod was in the study, doing his job in a methodical, professional way, Hamish returned from his walk and joined his wife in the sitting-room. He took up the *Observer* magazine section and, with only a vague

74

murmur about the dishevelled state she had left it in, began to look at the reviews.

He found it difficult to concentrate, and even the prose of Philip Toynbee and Angus Wilson floated above his consciousness like fat white clouds. Then he noticed a headline – 'The Anatomy of Truth' – and his attention was caught. It prefaced an article ostensibly about a new book by J. B. Priestley, but the writer had gone off on a tack of his own.

'In the maze of modern materialistic propaganda, which hammers at our minds from newspapers and television, the radio and the cinema, it is hard to find and take hold of essential truth. There is continual conflict between the aims of big business and the aims of philosophy. There are so many pretty roads leading off from the straight, steep highway to truth. Here is the problem confronting writers. Do they tag along with fashion, with an eye to material gain, or do they write with a poet's eye firmly fixed on signposts indicating "Right" and "Wrong"? It is a problem resembling the problem of a detective. In a mass of facts gleaned from many individuals – each individual presenting his own actions and motives in the best possible light – he has to decide which facts are basic and therefore relevant and which are merely incidental and bound for a mental scrapheap.'

That's good, thought Hamish. I wish I had written that. Then it occurred to him to look at himself in truth, and his sad conclusion was that his character and talents made him unfitted to be either a poet or a detective.

He looked across at his wife, who was reading the Dilys Powell article in the *Sunday Times*. She glanced up fleetingly and smiled. At least I have Janet, he told himself.

And while Hamish was wrestling with truth, old Peggy McAllister at last made up her mind to knock on Bruce's door.

5

(1)

IN the early nineteenth century, when a sailing vessel called *The Black Wherry* sailed regularly between Antrim and Kintyre, an Irish labourer and his wife crossed from Cushendun to Breckadale for the potato-gathering. They liked the place and settled in a shack down 'Teapot Lane', where they raised a large family. The 'Irish McAllisters' soon became well known in the district.

Old Peggy was a great grand-daughter of Seumas, who had disembarked at the jetty under Duncraig. Her mother had been the daughter of a shepherd born in North Uist, and this stream of Highland blood, mingling with the Irish, had brought her an inescapable heritage of superstition. It had also brought her the gifts of friendliness and physical strength.

It was as well that she possessed the latter, for she had never married and most of her life had been spent in farm-service, mucking out byres, lifting and cleaning

77

heavy milk-churns, thinning turnips on her knees in summer and shawing them with bent back in the sleet-filled days of winter. Stooped shoulders and an arthritic gait were evidence of past hardships, but she seldom visited the doctor.

For several years now, since passing the age of seventy, she had done no regular work. She lived alone in a Council house in the village – next door to the McRaes – and augmented her Old Age pension by letting part of her premises to summer visitors willing to do their own cooking. At times she did washings for chosen customers, one of whom was Bruce.

Between the almost illiterate old woman and the highly literate young man there existed sympathy and understanding. Amongst her neighbours, Peggy was reputed to have the second sight. Sometimes Bruce's writings gave people the same uncomfortable vision of things not yet completely understood. The common denominator may have been a highly developed Celtic imagination which made them sib to each other.

She knocked and waited. Her thin, wrinkled face, coloured like the tea she drank at all hours of the day and night, was rapt with anxiety. Her knuckled hands sought refuge in the ends of her shawl.

Bruce opened the door and looked at her with surprise. 'Peggy! Peggy, what is it?'

'Please excuse me, Mr. Cattanach. I have been keeping something to myself all day. In the end I made up my mind to come and tell you.'

'Of course. You did right.'

His voice was gentle, and as he put an arm about her and drew her inside, she clutched his free hand, venturing a small twisted smile.

He made her sit in his own favourite high-backed chair. 'I'm afraid the room's in a terrible mess. I didn't even light the stove this morning.'

She nodded several times, settling her skirts about her legs. 'You would have other things to worry you.'

'I had – yes. But – er – would you like a cup of tea? I'll plug in the kettle and—' He stopped, realising that she wasn't listening. 'What's the matter? What are you looking at?'

'The camans up there. The crossed camans above the mantelpiece.'

'My shinty sticks. You've seen them before, dozens of times. I had them at the University – remember I told you.'

'Ay. Sheena told me, too.'

He sat down in front of her on a cane-bottomed stool, his still unshaven chin supported by his hands, elbows on his wide-spread knees. 'You look as if they frightened you?' he said.

'No. It's just something that came into my mind. Sheena is a good girl, Mr. Cattanach. A fine girl.'

He was used to her moods and swerving flights of thought. He was also willing – more than willing, in fact – to talk about Sheena. 'The finest girl in the world,' he answered quickly. 'She is your neighbour. You ought to know.'

'When she talks of you, her eyes are like stars and she

79

is beautiful. I was hoping . . .' The thin voice quavered out; but she kept looking into his face as if eager to find the answer to a riddle.

'I was hoping, too,' he said.

'But last night – last night you had a quarrel?'

He covered his eyes with the palms of his hands. 'It was my fault. I call myself a poet – I should know how a woman feels. And yet—'

'And yet your love betrayed you?'

He lowered his hands. 'I think so. How did you know we had a quarrel?'

'This morning she brought my bottle of milk from the shop, as she always does. Her eyes were red with crying.'

'I didn't mean to hurt her.'

'I know you didn't, *laochain*. It is the way of young people in love. There are tears and accusations and angry words, but soon the laughter comes again.' Then unexpectedly, she leant forward and caught his hands. 'But that is not why I have come to see you, Mr. Cattanach.'

'What's troubling you?' he said.

'Come closer.'

'Yes?'

She glanced round, like a witch expecting priests. She said, 'There is something that I know about the murder.'

'What?'

'I'm afraid to tell it, in case they make fun of me.' Her eyes were anxious again. 'The police, I mean – and those who were his friends.'

'I shan't make fun of you.'

'I know. You are the only one I could think of who might understand.'

'Go on.'

She straightened up in the chair, gathering the ends of her shawl about her breast. Her expression changed. It seemed as if she was looking at something above and behind him.

'Last night it happened. I had been gathering fire-wood, out there on the shore. Nearly eleven o'clock it was, with the darkness coming down like a blanket. I was going home by way of the wee knoll above the golf green at the burn, when suddenly I heard them – the Hammers of Fingal – and I saw the sparks from the anvil flying up against the sky.' Her voice rose. 'I ran, Mr. Cattanach – at my age I ran – because I knew that someone in Breckadale was needing a coffin.'

Through the open window came the loud murmur of the sea. He found that he had been concentrating so hard on what she was saying that his muscles were stiffening. He tried to relax.

She bent forward again and put her fingers against his cheek. 'You – you believe me?' she said.

'I believe you.'

'It is true. I saw them.' She was excited now, and vehement. 'Bright sparks, with the blue of fire in them.'

He patted her knees and stood up. In a voice which he hoped sounded brisk and reassuring, he said, 'Don't worry, Peggy. You did the right thing coming here. I'll tell the police.'

81

'When will you tell them?'

'In a minute or two. I'll phone Inspector MacLeod at Mr. Heathergill's house.'

'Maybe Inspector MacLeod will make fun of *you*?'

'I don't think so. He's not that way inclined.' His smile brought the glimmer of a smile in return. 'Now then – now that you've told me everything – what about that cup of tea?'

'Very well.' As he filled the kettle, her smile grew broader. 'Sheena says I am always drinking tea and ruining my complexion!'

'She says much the same about me – only in my case it's the beer she's referring to. She'll just have to get used to our habits, won't she?'

'That's true. People never really change. It's the way we look at them that changes. Ay, she'll just have to get used to us, *laochain*.'

(2)

Supported by his two heavy thorn walking-sticks, John McRae hobbled in from the garden, where he had been weeding a plot of roses. It was a quarter to five and time for tea, because in about half-an-hour Sheena would be going off to her work at the hotel.

She had laid the table in the sitting-room. Generally they had their meals in the kitchen, but this was a Sunday when special rules favoured by her mother, who had died six years ago, were still observed.

As he sat down slowly and carefully, she came in with the teapot. 'Well, Dad – punctual as usual.'

'I'd get my head in my hands if I wasn't!'

He tried to make cheerful conversation, but he soon discovered that she was listening with only half an ear. She had been the same all day, and it worried him.

As he stretched forward to crack open his boiled egg, a stab of pain ran through his back, but he camouflaged his discomfort. As a young fisherman making a home for his wife and small daughter, he had been brash, impulsive and, at times, quick-tempered. But the death of his wife and the accident which left him fit only for making creels and repairing nets for others had doused the fires, turning brashness into quiet and temper into patience.

He was proud of Sheena, though he seldom told her so. She was good-looking and, even to his inexpert eye, knowledgeable about her clothes. Domestically, she was capable and kind and popular with the neighbours. Socially, she was inclined to be a little shy, but she liked dancing and only the week before had described to him in gay detail how she'd won a Twist competition in Kinloch, partnered by young Bruce Cattanach. With it all, he had found in her a certain determined Puritanism which had also been characteristic of her mother.

His one regret was that after taking five Highers in Kinloch Grammar School she hadn't gone on to the University. But that had been the summer her mother had taken ill, and somehow, after the funeral in the autumn, he had lacked the courage to oppose her decision to stay at home and keep house for him. Then he had met with his accident. . . .

Easing himself into a more comfortable position, he began to spoon out the contents of his egg. He saw that she was only picking at a biscuit and that after a minute or two she left the remains of it on her plate and lit a cigarette.

'What's up, lass? Tell me.'

'Nothing, Dad.'

'Is it this – this murder business?'

'No. . . . Well, it is, in a way. But—'

'Is young Cattanach mixed up in it?'

'Of course not!' She spoke sharply, with a flush spreading on her cheeks. 'Why should he be?'

He felt the pain again, but was determined not to show it. 'You're unhappy, lass,' he said quietly.

She took a gulp of tea and nodded. All day she had been unhappy – all day and all last night, after what had taken place between Bruce and herself; and since early morning, when she had been told by Mrs. Allison in the shop about the discovery of McDermott's body, her unhappiness had been mixed with a surging panic that was hard to suppress. She would have liked to talk about all this with her father but shrank from the emotional effort. Better to keep control. Better to hide from him that her mind was a whirling churn of love and fear and contempt for her own inadequacy.

Bruce was unreasonably jealous. That had been the cause of everything. Or was it? Last night she had been casting about stupidly for a sign that he loved her without strings or conditions. But had that been fair? Was it not her own love that lacked trust? How often

84

she had heard old Peggy say, 'Love's not a brittle tree that cracks with every wind that blows.' Had she failed Bruce at the very time he needed her to be strong?

And now, adding to her confusion, there was this matter of the photograph. . . .

She said, 'Don't you worry, Dad. Maybe it's just that I'm a bit nervous. Remember the policeman that called this morning. He had a message to say that Inspector MacLeod wants to see me at the Heathergills' house. I have to call there in about fifteen minutes – on my way to the hotel.'

'Why should the inspector want to see *you*?'

'Well, I expect he's checking up on everybody McDermott spoke to, in case he said anything that might point to – to the murderer.'

He knew that this was only the upper crust of the iceberg – that she was concealing the main cause of her distress. 'Sheena,' he said, 'if there's anything between you and Cattanach, don't let me be a hindrance to you, I'm well able to look after myself – in my own way.'

She got up quickly, crossed over and kissed the bald patch on the back of his grizzled head. 'Thanks for that, Dad. And you can start looking after yourself right now by clearing the table and doing the washing-up. I've got to run. I'd hate to be arrested for contempt of court or something!'

They laughed together. But their laughter didn't quite ring true.

She took her dust-coat on her arm against the walk home from the hotel in the cool dusk. Avoiding the short cut through the golf course, she went by the main road, past the rows of Council houses, past the Coast-guard Station and along the narrow road which led down past bordering hedges of hawthorn to the shore.

At the junction of the golf course road she stopped for a minute to talk with a group of village boys. Knowing she worked at the hotel, they asked her about the man who had been killed, but she could tell them nothing they didn't already know.

Two young men in a sports car – guests at the hotel – offered her a lift, but she explained that in the meantime she was only going as far as the red-roofed bungalow, and they went off again, waving.

Where the road began to dip down above the shore she encountered a number of young people from the caravans on their way to the village – probably to buy cool drinks at the shop after their long and un-successful search in the afternoon sun. They stared at her, as if a smartly dressed girl who didn't belong to their holiday crowd was a kind of curiosity.

A few hundred yards from the Heathergills' gate she met the minister cycling back to the Manse after a christening in the glen. He was a young unmarried man in his first charge, but a powerful devotion to duty hadn't dimmed his eye for a pretty girl. In any case, besides asking for her father, it was his duty to glean from someone who had actually known the murdered man a few authentic details about an event that had ruined the Sabbath calm of his parish. But though Sheena was patient with his queries, time was passing and she had to excuse herself at last. He shook hands warmly and jumped on his bike. Looking back and raising his hat, he almost fell off as his front wheel wobbled.

'I'll need to watch out I'm not arrested for dangerous driving!' he called to her, with a slightly embarrassed laugh.

She smiled and waved. She liked him and wished she could have been more sociable. But she was about to be questioned by an inspector of police, and it was difficult to appear normal and natural.

Indeed, her walk down from the village had possessed for her a kind of nightmare unreality. Here in a place that she knew so well it was incredible that a man should have been savagely attacked and killed. Here amongst people that she knew so well it was incredible that a cruel murderer should be at large.

Hayricks and ripening cornfields absorbed the sunshine; the hawthorn filled the air with its waxy scent; the sea lazed and lapped around the rocks near Bruce's house across the bay, and on the other side of the channel the Mountains of Mourne rose up against the sky as they had done for a million years. On the beach, caravan children were building castles and squealing defiance at the cold water as they dipped their toes in it. From a farm-building behind the hotel came the electronic whine of a milking-machine engine.

Everything was the same, though as emotion heightened her perception it appeared to her rather more lovely and desirable than usual. Everything was the same – and yet beneath the pleasant surface there lay the ugliness of lust and death.

The high heels of her shoes teetered in the gravel of the driveway, and her heart began to beat so fast that it almost stifled her. She was glad that it was Mrs. Heathergill who opened the door. The sympathetic voice and firm hand on her arm helped to make her feel less frightened.

'Inspector MacLeod? Oh, he's nice – quite human and domesticated. You don't need to be afraid of him.'

Normality again. How much she wished she had never spoken to Finlay McDermott or seen the warm light of masculine interest in his eyes. How much she wished that Saturday night had never happened. Then she, too, could have been normal and ordinary, able to match Mrs. Heathergill's affectionate greeting with affection of her own.

But when MacLeod gallantly bowed her into the chair in front of the desk and lit a cigarette for her, she found, unexpectedly, that the feeling of unreality began to ebb. He was as normal as a fencing-post, and soon she was answering his questions with a fair amount of confidence.

As well as she remembered she described the events of Friday night in the cocktail bar – the talk about the golf match that had been arranged between Colin Campbell and the two other men; Bruce's annoyance when McDermott had tried to kiss her – and the violent outburst of anger between them, smothered almost at once when the sound of the Hammers of Fingal had come in through the open window.

'It was McDermott who opened the window?'

'Yes. It had become warm and stuffy.'

'Tell me, Miss McRae' – he smiled encouragingly – 'this was the first time you'd met him?'

'Yes.'

'You treated him as you'd treat any other guest?'

She flushed. 'Certainly, Inspector.'

'Quite. I have no doubt that in your job you meet plenty of his sort. The lady-killing type,' he expanded, weightily.

She nodded.

'And you regard them as a kind of – er – occupational hazard?'

She couldn't help smiling. 'Yes. I wish Bruce could see it like that.'

'I'm a bit older than Mr. Cattanach,' he said, returning her smile. 'And maybe a bit wiser in the ways of the world. Now, Miss McRae – Saturday night. I have to find out what people were doing between approximately ten-thirty and eleven.'

'Was that when—'

'Ay. Where were you at that time?'

'With Bruce, among the dunes near his house.'

'When exactly did you meet him?'

'I – I'm not sure. Soon after a quarter past ten, I think.'

'And when did you say good night?'

Suddenly she was ready to cry again. The memory of

a meeting that had begun in love and ended in bitterness came surging up from the depths in which she had been trying to hide it. The sad futility of it all threatened to overwhelm her.

MacLeod saw that her eyes were full of tears and that her lower lip was trembling. Having a daughter of his own who frequently quarrelled with her young man, he recognized the signs.

Gently he repeated, 'When did you say good night?'

She made a choking effort to regain control. 'Shortly before – shortly before eleven it must have been. I went home across the golf course – by myself,' she added, bleakly – 'and got in at about ten past. I noticed the time on my alarm when I set it for the morning.'

'I see. Ay, that fits in with what Mr. Cattanach told me.'

But he didn't tell you that I nagged him into a quarrel, she thought miserably. He didn't tell you that I was a fool, confusing the romance of a magazine story with the reality of love. He didn't tell you that he's all alone now, thinking that I don't care. . . .

'On your way across the golf course, did you meet anyone?'

She took a long drag at her cigarette. 'Nobody,' she said.

'You heard nothing? Saw nothing?'

'No. Except, of course, that the Hammers of Fingal were very loud. I – I was scared. In fact, I ran some of the way.'

'H'm. One more point. I'm sure there's a simple

explanation, but how did McDermott come to have a snapshot of you in the pocket of his golf jacket?'

She braced herself and grew still. The moment had come, as she had known it must come sooner or later.

She took a long breath and answered, carefully, 'Just before he and Mr. Marlin went out to golf – on Saturday evening, after their high-tea – he came into the bar for a drink. The porter – Patrick McConnachie – was collecting an order for the lounge, and I was showing him some photos Bruce had taken and left with me the night before. Mr. McDermott saw the one – the one you found. He wanted me to let him have it, and when I refused he snatched it out of my hand and went away, laughing.'

'That was all, Miss McRae?'

'That was all.'

He nodded and rose solidly to his feet. 'I don't think there's anything more – not in the meantime. Thank you for being so frank with me. I may see you later this evening in the hotel – in more of a social capacity.'

She got up, too, folding her dust-coat over her arm. After a momentary pause and trying to keep her voice steady, she said, 'Can you tell me, does Bruce know about the photo?'

'He does. He and Mr. Heathergill were there, you know, when we examined the body.'

So her fear had come true, and she had to face it. 'Did he seem surprised?'

She was painfully tense, and MacLeod, aware again of

her likeness to his daughter, suddenly realised that he was a man as well as a policeman. 'Not in the least,' he replied, with a show of casual disinterest. 'As a matter of fact, when he identified you in the snapshot he said you were the girl he intended to marry.'

She looked up at him, the muscles in her face relaxing, a brightness in her eyes dispersing the tears. 'Bruce said that?'

'Ay. Very emphatically, too. I must say I admired him for it – the circumstances being what they were. Though, of course, now that I know you better, I can see that his faith in you wasn't such a remarkable thing after all.'

Without warning she caught his big hand in both of hers and squeezed it. 'Oh, thank you, Inspector!'

Then, with a whirl of her coat and a flash of nylon-clad legs, she was at the door, smiling back at him as she opened it and went out.

He squared his shoulders and scratched his head.

He was amazed at himself. It had been a good feeling to play Santa Claus. But now he was beginning to worry in case the gift he had given this nice, attractive girl might soon, if his instincts were at fault, be snatched away from her again.

If that should happen, then he had just done something infinitely cruel.

(3)

Toiling at the sink, both Hamish and MacLeod were in their shirt-sleeves and wearing aprons.

Janet came briskly into the kitchen with a tray of crockery. 'Well, how goes the washing-up?'

'Fine. Just fine,' replied her husband drably.

Depositing her load in the soapy hot water, she said, 'You wield a pretty dish-cloth, Inspector.'

'Och, I'm used to it. My missus keeps me at it.'

'Take note,' she said to Hamish.

He ignored her.

'Mind you,' the inspector continued. 'I'm not always working in the house – like an author does. In my case it's maybe more of a change.'

'How you men stick together!' She sighed and shook her head before suddenly exclaiming, 'Oh, Hamish, don't look so utterly helpless! You'll never dry a plate by just dabbing at it like that!'

'I'm doing my best,' he told her with dignity.

'All right.' She tried not to giggle as she went towards the door. 'I'll be back in due course with the tea-cups.'

Hamish waited until she had disappeared. Then, lowering his voice, he said, 'Look, Duncan, I hope you don't mind all this – I mean, being conscripted as a washer-upper?'

'Not in the least.' MacLeod had been tired and somewhat on edge after the long day's work, but a dram and a tasty meal had restored his even humour. 'Murderers may come and murderers may go, but dish-washing goes on for ever.'

'She's not generally so – so stubborn,' explained Hamish, instinctively loyal. 'She's just a little upset – about this murder business.'

'Aren't we all!'

Hamish went on polishing an already dry and polished plate. 'By the way,' he said presently, as if struck by an unimportant thought, 'that phone-call you had at tea-time. It – er – it seemed to worry you?'

'It puzzled me. Looks now as if we're dealing with ghosts!'

'Eh?' The plate was held high in a mime of avid curiosity.

'Bruce Cattanach tells me he's just had a visit from a friend of his – that old wife in the village, Peggy McAllister.'

'What on earth has Peggy got to do with it?'

'Last night she was close to the scene of the murder – between half-past ten and eleven o'clock. In her own words she heard the Hammers of Fingal and saw sparks from the anvil flying up against the sky.'

The plate fell from Hamish's fingers, splintering on the floor, but for a second he seemed unaware of the calamity. Then suddenly his almost vacant expression became one of consternation.

'Oh, Lord help us! Now I'm for it!' he muttered.

'Maybe she didn't hear,' MacLeod soothed him, bending down to pick up the pieces.

'Don't kid yourself. She has everything counted.'

The inspector got up. 'Where do I put this lot?'

'In the refuse bucket – under the sink.'

MacLeod toed the lever which raised the lid and dropped the fragments in.

He began to rinse another plate. 'What old Peggy said startled you, eh?'

'It certainly did.'

'She's a wee bit strange, I gather. Second sight and all that nonsense. Think she was making it up?'

Hamish went on drying, absently and ineffectively. 'No, I don't. Peggy behaves oddly at times, but she doesn't make things up. I know her.'

'H'm. Mind you, it's beginning to look as if this murder *was* committed by a ghost. Thanks to that phone call at nine minutes to eleven, Marlin and young Campbell have fool-proof alibis.'

Hamish had a secret feeling of satisfaction, for this was the kind of conversation he had been angling for all day. 'So it seems,' he said, still trying to sound casual.

'How d'you mean, so it seems?' MacLeod was abruptly and unexpectedly irritable. 'I deal in facts, not in airy-fairy stuff about legendary blacksmiths!'

'I know, Duncan. I know.'

Somewhat mollified, the inspector went on, 'By the same token, Bruce Cattanach and Sheena McRae are out of the reckoning, too. At the time of the murder they were together among the sand-dunes – necking. Or so they tell me.'

Hamish frowned and said, 'There's just one thing.'

'Ay?'

'This afternoon Colin told me he brought back Marlin's 9-iron. Did he tell you why he borrowed it in the first place?'

'I didn't ask. To get out of an awkward lie among the

whins, presumably. I took it he hadn't a heavy enough club of his own.'

Hamish assumed a portentous expression. 'That's not quite right,' he said, enjoyably taking on the role of an intellectual Dr. Watson. 'Colin explained to me that he borrowed it because the only way of playing the ball was left-handed. Marlin, you see, is left-handed. All his clubs are left-handed.'

'A *cioteach*, eh!' MacLeod's interest was suitably lively. For a time he stood silent and still, glowering at another dripping plate in his hand. Then he put it down and said, quietly, 'You know, Hamish, I have an idea that someone is trying to fool me!'

Distantly, the telephone began to ring.

A few seconds later Janet came hurrying into the kitchen. 'It's for you, Inspector. Another newspaper.'

6

(1)

THE newspapers had got on to the story late in the afternoon, following the receipt of agency wires written originally by the *Kinloch Courier* man. Inspector Mac-Leod was tracked to Hamish's house, and now the phone had begun to ring every few minutes.

After tea the telephone assault increased in violence, and Hamish was distressed to find that Janet's reactions became steadily more inimical. He didn't object to the excitement himself, and he wished – vainly – that she could have shared his tolerant outlook.

When their guest departed for the hotel about eight o'clock, however, the atmosphere grew calmer. Hamish produced the box of chocolates he had bought that morning and suggested that they should watch the play on television. Gradually signs began to accumulate that his wife's good humour was returning.

Two minutes after the play started the telephone rang again.

'Hell!' he said, looking to her for sympathy. None was forthcoming.

He went out into the study and lifted the receiver. It was a long-distance call from the editor of the Scottish edition of the *Clarion*, whom he had met at a literary luncheon in Glasgow some weeks before and who now wanted him to write a series of special articles on the murder case.

'It's a natural, old boy. Hamish Heathergill, the famous crime writer, reports daily on a crime committed on his own doorstep. A thousand words tonight, seven hundred tomorrow and seven hundred the day after, provided there hasn't been an arrest before then. We'll pay you well, of course.' And he mentioned a fee that made Hamish pause and consider.

The editor went on, 'Nobody's been charged yet, have they?'

'Not yet.'

'Are the police on to anybody?'

'I wouldn't know.'

'Well, you get to know, old boy. And tell us all about it. Good publicity for your books.'

But Hamish wasn't thinking about publicity or even about the money. He said, 'Look, it's good of you to suggest this, but wouldn't it be doing a real reporter out of a job?'

'Come off it! Our staff man's on the way down to Breckadale by car at this moment. Along with a photographer. He'll be sending in stuff of his own – factual stuff – and I've instructed him to give you any technical assistance you may need. He's thrilled at the idea of working alongside the great man.'

Hamish was used to this kind of flattery when some-body wanted his help, and he remained unmoved. But it suddenly occured to him that if he accepted the job he would be in a much stronger position in regard to Duncan. In fact, he'd be able to put any kind of awkward question he liked, without fear of being misunderstood.

'Well, in that case—' he began.

'Good man!' said the editor. 'Give us a thousand words in about an hour from now to catch the first edition. By that time MacTaggart should have contacted you. Our staff man.'

The telephone clicked, and Hamish was left alone with his thoughts – and Janet.

But he was a skilled tradesman and, when the necessity arose, could clear his mind of distractions and work at speed. By ten o'clock his piece had been written and phoned through to the *Clarion* office. It contained plenty of drama and local colour – which was what the editor had bargained for – but only one official 'quote', a single sentence wrung with difficulty from Duncan over the phone. 'Inquiries are being made, and the Argyllshire police are confident that an arrest will soon be made.'

Then, physically a little weary but mentally ex-hilarated, Hamish clapped MacTaggart on the back and said, 'Before you join your cameraman at the hotel let's have a dram. We need it. I – er – I think my wife is bringing in some coffee and sandwiches.'

The final statement caused a resurgence of guilt; but

on this occasion he needn't have worried. Janet had taken a liking to the young reporter, who was quiet, efficient and polite – and called Hamish 'Sir'.

Indeed, at about ten o'clock, when they were alone again, she came and sat on the arm of his chair, showing every sign of normal wifely affection. 'You look tired, dear. Don't you think we ought to go to bed?'

'I'll maybe read for half-an-hour. The "wind down" treatment. But you go, Janet. It's been a rotten day for you.'

'Yes. Your Inspector MacLeod is inclined to be overpowering, in large doses.'

'He's a fine man. Straight as a die. Dependable, like all Skyemen.'

'Not very forthcoming, is he?'

'Well, he's a policeman.'

'How is he getting on? Does he suspect anyone?'

'If he does, he hasn't told me. You know, this morning I believed he might take me on as a kind of amateur assistant. An audience to try out his theories on. But that only happens in books, it seems. Duncan's pukka and official. We're friends – but I'm not another policeman.'

'They're talking in the village about Fingal's Cave. About something that may have come out of it last night.'

'Who told you?'

'Wee Mary Allison from the shop. I phoned up for some fresh coffee, and her mother sent her down on her bike. Everybody is sure it was a hammer that killed McDermott. A blacksmith's hammer.'

100

'The usual superstitious rubbish! I expect old Peggy's mainly responsible for it.'

'I wish it *could* be put down to superstition.'

'The murder, you mean?'

'Yes. I hate to imagine that somebody we know is a killer.'

'We may not know him.'

'I think we do,' she said with a shiver.

(2)

Presently, however, the mood passed, and she got up, yawning. 'Well, darling, I'm off. I've just about had enough for one day. Be sure to lock up before you come.'

'Right, Janet. I shan't be long.'

His mind was still active after the bout of writing. He took *The Age of Reason* from his bookcase and began to read the chapter on Samuel Johnson entitled 'Common Sense'. It seemed an appropriate exercise. But not even Harold Nicholson's beguiling prose could fully engage his attention. Soon his thoughts were wandering.

As he reviewed the events of the day and the meagre information he had prised from Duncan, he became more and more restless and anxious. Something was nagging at the back of his mind – something he couldn't quite pin down: a statement, perhaps, that didn't ring true, or a fact that broke the basic pattern of the jig-saw.

He got up and paced the room. It was nearly eleven o'clock, a quiet and lonely time at which he often gave birth to the best ideas for his books. Was an idea about to be born now, in connection with the murder?

He told himself to play it cool. You never forced ideas any more than you forced a golf shot. You let them simmer in the subconscious until suddenly, almost without you being aware of it, they boiled and bubbled over.

Then it came to him – what he believed in a moment of triumph might be the crux of the whole problem. *How long did it take to walk the distance between the hotel and the seventeenth green?*

He tried to work it out in his head, but the answer was a nebulous one. It could be ten minutes, or it could be twenty, depending on how fast you walked.

Excitement fluttered in his diaphragm. It was essential that he should know the truth. If he didn't know it that very night he'd never rest. . . .

He looked quietly into the bedroom, but already Janet was asleep, her dark hair spread on the pillow. He had a moment of desire for the comfort of bed, but he was also aware that it was a comfort he could never appreciate if he dodged the persistent question in his brain.

After bolting the front door on the inside, he went out through the kitchen and locked the door behind him, pocketing the key.

The night was fairly dark, for the moon hadn't yet appeared like a stackyard fire above the horizon, but the stars were all visible, and he had no difficulty in finding his way. A thin wind, salt-scented, was blowing from the south-east.

Some lights were still on in the hotel, but the distant

farms were in darkness and in the village only the street lamps were burning. Somewhere on the high ground behind the hotel a tom cat screeched a challenge.

Hamish disliked dallying. If he had a job to do he tended to do it quickly, in order that as soon as possible he might enjoy the reward of an easy conscience. Like a harrier, therefore, he strode along the road and up towards the hotel.

No one was about. In the dim radiance of the front door light he looked at his wrist-watch and found the time to be exactly thirteen minutes past eleven. Then he turned and, by way of a side gate, began to walk briskly through the fields in the direction of the burn and the seventeenth green.

It was a short-cut often used by visitors. Running through clumps of clover, the well-beaten path presented far more hazards in the dark than it did in daylight. Cow-dung, for instance. And cows themselves. Before he reached the main road crossing he had trodden in dung twice and stumbled into one old cow breathing heavily as she chewed her cud. He swore to himself. Wiping his shoes clean with thick handfuls of grass, he thought wistfully of Janet warm in bed.

On the golf course the going was easier. He passed the clubhouse, its blank windows reflecting the stars, and bore left on to the track which led through the eighteenth fairway to the Golfers' Bridge. Where the Con met the sea under Duncraig, small waves were making a fuss; but the Hammers of Fingal were silent.

The close-cut turf was tender beneath his feet. He

began to recover some of the eagerness that had left him during his smelly passage through the cow-dung. In a few minutes he would reach the seventeenth green. Then a glance at his watch would reveal the truth and he could make a beeline for home.

But the knowledge he sought was to be denied him. As he climbed towards the ridge overlooking the green a shadow appeared in front – a formless shadow which at first appeared gigantic. He stopped and stared and forgot about times and distances.

Then he saw that it was an old woman wrapped in shawls who sat on the red box marking the eighteenth tee.

'Peggy!' he exclaimed, his voice sharpened by relief and surprise.

She got up stiffly and moved towards him. 'I have been waiting to see if they would come,' she whispered. 'Mr. Cattanach believes me, but not the inspector.'

'What are you talking about?'

'He questioned me tonight. Kind and gentle he was, being from Skye, and he didn't make a mock of me. But I knew he had his doubts. I had doubts myself. That's why I made up my mind to keep watch and see if they would come again.'

'The sparks from the anvil, you mean?'

'Ay. And the three great smiths with their yellow hair.'

He put an arm about her shoulders. They stood together just beneath the highest part of the ridge. Beyond it, in the starlight, they could make out the black bulk of Duncraig, the glint of water at the mouth of the Con, and, much nearer, the tops of the poles

104

which carried the telephone wires to Bruce's house. The green itself was hidden.

'This is where I stood last night and saw – what I saw, Mr. Heathergill.'

He had a feeling that he'd stumbled on something far more important than mere timings. 'What exactly did you see?' he asked.

'I saw the smiths coming out of the cave – great giants with terrible eyes. Then I heard the sound of their hammers – beating, beating, beating – and the sparks flew up, high above the ridge.'

'You *saw* the smiths?'

'Ay.'

'All three of them?'

'Well, one at any rate. He came towards the burn, twelve feet tall—'

'But Peggy—'

'His head was above the ridge, so he must have been twelve feet tall. And when he swung the hammer it thudded on the anvil and the sparks rose up into the sky.'

He did his best to be patient. This was Peggy in one of her most exasperating moods – 'away with the fairies', as Janet put it. And yet – and yet Peggy was no liar. She had seen *something*. This he knew.

He took a deep breath and said, 'You told Bruce and the inspector about the sparks. Did you tell them you'd seen Fingal's smith as well?'

'I didn't, Mr. Heathergill. I was confused and afraid. Because . . . because . . .'

105

'Because you couldn't be certain what was true and what was imaginary?'

'That's right. It was working in my head – the whole story. The big men in the cave, with their glistening bodies and their curly hair. I heard the hammering and could see them in the cave, swinging and heaving in the light of the furnace. And then – then one of them appeared, and I couldn't be sure if he was only in my mind. But now I am sure. I saw him yonder, towering above the ridge.'

Hamish scorned superstition; but now in the lowering dark his muscles were prickling. For what seemed a long time he remained with his arm about old Peggy. But they saw nothing, except in the eye of imagination.

At last, gently, he said, 'It's getting cold. Let's go home.'

She nodded. 'I'm ready. My thoughts are calm again. I know now that I was not mistaken.'

He accompanied her to the village, walking slowly and sometimes supporting her on rough parts of the road, and saw her in at her own front door.

'Was Fingal angry with Mr. McDermott? Did he send his smiths to kill him?'

He patted her arm and said, 'Don't go on worrying about it. Leave that to the inspector. I'll tell him what you said.'

(3)

Quietly he let himself into the bungalow. By now the original reason for his night journey had been forgotten, and his mind was a racing confusion of dim, half-formed theories about the murder and of brilliant sentences for use in the article he had decided to write tomorrow for the *Clarion*. His first piece had been too prosaic – that was obvious in retrospect. But now he could see inch-high headlines: 'THE HAMMERS OF FINGAL by HAMISH HEATHERGILL. ANCIENT LEGEND COMES TO LIFE IN OLD WOMAN'S STORY.'

Janet appeared to be still asleep. He undressed quietly, and as he took off his watch and wound it he saw that he had been away for little more than an hour. In turn he felt happy, tense, elated and anxious. It was a state in which he often found himself – a writer's state – which could be resolved only by the act of writing or in sleep.

He put out the light and got into bed.

Janet stirred and turned towards him, sleepily. 'What's the time, darling?'

'Just after twelve.'

'I thought I heard you lock up ages ago.'

He would explain in the morning, he decided, drawing her close and kissing her.

She snuggled against him. 'What's all this? Don't you want to sleep?'

'Not yet, Janet.'

'Neither do I,' she whispered.

Later he did sleep, soothed and content in body and in spirit. His wife slept, too, lying comfortably in the crook of his arm.

7

(1)

SHORTLY after ten o'clock in the morning, calm and smoothly shaved, Inspector MacLeod called at the bungalow. By then Hamish had made a quick draft of his *Clarion* article, which included a description of his encounter with old Peggy.

Fired with the joy of completed composition, he showed it to Duncan. 'One of the best things I've written,' he said enthusiastically.

Knowing an author's mind in general, and Hamish's in particular, Duncan discounted the enthusiasm. As he began to read, however, his own imagination flickered, though his expression gave nothing away.

Returning the script, he said, 'Very good indeed. That should take a trick.'

Hamish appreciated the compliment to his literary skill, but was disappointed that his friend should be so non-committal about the contents of the article.

He said, 'In my opinion, Duncan, Peggy saw the murder actually happening.'

Sitting down on the edge of the desk in the study, the inspector shrugged broad shoulders. 'I had a session with her last night, soon after I left you. Seems to me you can't place too much reliance on what she says.'

'In a way you're right. She leaves gaps – and her Gaelic imagination distorts a number of the details. But I firmly believe that her account of what she saw is essentially true, in the same way as an impressionist picture is true. You translate the artist's idiom into your own and discover reality.'

'H'm. That's a bit high-falutin' for me!' MacLeod's heavy face broke into a smile. 'Tell you what,' he continued, briskly, 'my boys have gone back to Kinloch to do a spot of technical work, and at the moment I'm at a loose end. What about taking me to see this famous cave that all the fuss is about?'

'All right. We can't get to it by land, of course, because it's at the bottom of that fearsome cliff behind Duncraig. But I'll find out if Dan the Dooker is available to take us in his boat – and I expect he will be, because I saw him at his lobster-creels before breakfast. But in return, Duncan, I'd like you to promise me something.'

'A *quid pro quo*, eh?'

'Something like that. Before I phone this article to the *Clarion* tonight, will you promise to tell me if an arrest is imminent?'

'How d'you know an arrest won't actually have been made before tonight?'

Hamish frowned. 'Well, good enough. If that happens I want an exclusive interview. Though it would mean cutting out most of the stuff about the Hammers of Fingal,' he added, unable to hide his loathing of the prospect.

'It's a promise,' laughed the inspector, getting up and clapping him on the back. 'But you know,' he went on, 'you authors are a queer lot. You're always trying to manipulate the facts in order to make a good story. I don't blame you, mind – it's your living. But it's dangerous. You concentrate on glamour and romance and tend to overlook the plain, hard facts. Especially the plain, hard facts of human nature.'

Hamish smiled. After a moment he said, 'What was that in aid of?'

'Just a fly to stick on the wall,' returned his friend. 'Come on now – I feel in the mood for a breath of fresh air. And for a dose of your stimulating conversation. You may be a romantic, Hamish, but romance is always far more interesting than dull detective work. Even to a policeman.'

'Right. I'll tell Janet where we're going. She's expecting you for lunch, by the way. I hope you'll come?'

'With pleasure.'

'Good. I'm glad you didn't answer that one with another riddle!'

(2)

Hamish took his car.

They found Dan the Dooker in a shed behind his

cottage in the village. Surrounded by supple hazel-wands and pots of steaming tar, he was busy repairing lobster-creels.

Most people in Breckadale believed that Dan Morrison was over ninety, though a few, themselves competing for the title of oldest inhabitant, were quick to deny this, putting his age at a mere eighty-six. Whatever the truth might be – and that lay buried in some obscure parish register in his native Islay – his step was still springy and his eyes retained the clarity of a frosty sky.

In his youth, according to himself, he had sailed before the mast; and one of the stories he regularly told Hamish concerned a hurricane encountered by his ship off Cape Horn. The waves had been so high, he said, that when a passing vessel was caught up, bow and stern, he'd actually seen the barren land of Terra del Fuego beneath her dripping keel. . . .

Though the morning was warm – and getting warmer – he wore a bulky blue guernsey and his customary red woollen cap. This cap, he often explained, had been presented to him during the first World War by the crew of a Belgian trawler wrecked on Duncraig, whose rescue he had accomplished single handed and with great heroism. On one occasion Hamish had examined the cap and found a tag inside which mentioned a shop in Kinloch, but this may have been an irrelevant detail.

Hamish introduced the inspector, and Dan, always at his best with V.I.P.'s, immediately expressed his willingness to take them to the cave in his motor-boat.

'No bother at all, at all,' he assured them, adding in a hoarse whisper, 'It'll be in connection with the murder, eh?'

'In a way,' conceded MacLeod.

'Ay, well, I don't hold with all them yarns about Fingal's smiths myself. Though, mind you, it's a peculiar coincidence that the last time I had a policeman in my boat it was to investigate a body found in that very cave. A sailor he was, from an American ship. Washed overboard – that's what they said – but man, if you'd seen the way his skull was bashed in you might have been thinking different. Of course, that was maybe fifty years ago, when the police weren't so efficient as they are nowadays.'

Partially concealed under a wiry grey stubble, his ruddy face expressed the wisdom and experience of the ages. He fumbled in his trousers' pocket and took out a battered cigarette-case, which with a dramatic gesture of dismay, he discovered to be empty. Almost guiltily, MacLeod produced his own case and offered it. After all, the efficiency of the modern police was at stake.

Hamish drove down through the golf course, parking the car above the dunes. As they walked towards Bruce's house and the jetty, children from the village and the caravans clamoured at their heels, demanding a sail in Dan's boat. He was obviously a great favourite, but this time, with an inspector of police in tow, he ordered them with gruff authority to 'beat it'. Reluctantly they did so, looking hurt and puzzled, as if a friendly dog had unexpectedly turned and growled at them.

The beach was dotted with small family groups, sun-bathing, playing cricket, building castles. A tall man with a bald head was walking on the firm sand at the edge of the tide, heading for the jetty.

'Marlin, isn't it?' said Hamish.

MacLeod nodded. 'I had a word with him at breakfast-time and hinted we might be going to see the cave. He appeared to be interested, so I told him to be around and on the look-out for us.'

'H'm. You're not as green as you're cabbage-looking, are you, Duncan?'

'It's a matter of training. Training and technique.'

They scrambled over the rocks, Dan the most sure-footed and spry of them all. His white, twelve-foot boat lay alongside the jetty, and as he nimbly climbed into her and began to prime the motor, Marlin joined the others on the flat concrete.

'Just in time,' MacLeod greeted him. 'Glad you made it.'

'Anything for a change.' Marlin's mood seemed to be as grey as his sweater. 'It's boring up there in the hotel, now that I'm – well, officially in mourning. I'll be glad when the funeral's over tomorrow and I can get away.'

MacLeod looked sympathetic. 'Didn't you tell me Mrs. McDermott would be arriving in the morning?'

'Yes.'

'That ought to ease the situation. You'll be taking her back to Glasgow in your car, I expect?'

'Very likely.'

Hamish had been keeping an eye on the old lifeboat

house, about a hundred yards away, but there was no sign of Bruce. Now, as Dan's ripe voice boomed up, requesting them to come aboard, he refocussed his attention and busied himself in casting off.

Uneasiness, however, still pricked him. Bruce was probably working inside, because his weekly review for Thursday's issue of the *Gazette* had to be posted first thing on a Tuesday. But the fact remained that he hadn't seen him since the previous morning, when their vigil beside the body had come to an end. What had been going on during the past twenty-four hours in that lonely, introspective mind – especially in regard to the snapshot of Sheena found in McDermott's pocket?

The motor spluttered into raucous life, and as the boat slid forward Dan swung her bow into the cool green swell outside Duncraig. Even though the sun was shining, the sea air had a chill in it, and the purpose of Dan's thick guernsey became apparent.

As they moved out to circle the reef, with the gulls trailing behind in a vain search for scraps, Duncraig loomed darkly above them, its red rock dark in shadow. To the left of it, however, they had a view of the Breckadale valley, wide and fertile, with the Con winding through like a silver ribbon carelessly discarded. In some of the fields tractors were moving towards the stackyards, hauling loads of hay. It was a guileless scene, pleasant and quiet, but Hamish remembered the old Gaelic saying, *Beware of the death that lurks in a fair meadow*, and found his spirit teetering on the brink of depression.

He was roused by a cheerful shout from Dan, 'Hey, Mr. Heathergill, the gentlemen here are wanting to know the history of the Rock. I'm telling them there's nobody knows it better than yourself.'

Depression was forgotten as he accepted the bait. He bent forward against the starboard gun'le and prepared to address MacLeod and Marlin, who were sitting together on the after thwart.

Some day, when he'd made his pile, he meant to write a non-commercial book about Duncraig entitled *A Hub of History*. He would begin – as he now began – with a description of its constituent Old Red Sandstone, formed of pebbles from the shore of a primeval lake gradually cemented together by sand and silt as the earth cooled. He would mention – as he now mentioned – that on its exposed surfaces there could still be found the fossil impressions of the trilobites, small extinct shellfish which three hundred million years ago were the highest form of life.

His theory, as he informed his small but attentive audience, was that the first men to see Duncraig had done so in 6000 B.C. – Mesolithic men from Ireland, with flint arrows and flint tools stuck in their reindeer belts. They were, he thought, the first human beings to settle in Kintyre after the Ice Age and almost certainly the first inhabitants of Scotland: middle Stone Age men – small and slant-eyed, terrified of the dark and of the monsters of the dark. They were followed by men of the Neolithic Age, then by men of the Bronze Age and the Iron Age, whose arrow-heads, drinking utensils and primitive tools had all been found near the Rock.

'In place of terror,' said Hamish, now happily in full stride, 'these later inhabitants were beginning to recognize an idea of love. And as proof of that I could show you a stone barrow up yonder above the hotel, where a few years ago archaeologists found some tiny coloured beads – the remains of a necklace placed in the grave of a child.'

After a moment he continued: 'According to an old legend, St. Columba and his disciples first paid a visit to Breckadale before going to Iona. In fact, they're supposed to have landed from their coracles on the beach back there. And it's significant that in the field behind my bungalow there's a well-preserved Druidical altar, complete with cup-marks and emblems of the sun. Because, you see, Columba was in part a Druid and built his new faith of love on the foundation of the old.'

A careless elbow on the tiller, Dan was listening with a satisfied smile. Clearly the two 'incomers' were impressed. Trust Mr. Heathergill to put it across. . . .

Marlin remained silent and lit another cigarette, but MacLeod said, 'Isn't there some kind of old ruin on the Rock itself?'

'Yes. The ruin of a MacDonald castle burnt to the ground in 1647 by invading Campbells. You can see the remains of the blackened and broken south wall – on the flat shoulder up there, just below the summit. The garrison was put to the sword – "every mother's son", according to the official account – and only the infant Lord of the Isles, James Ranald MacDonald, escaped

116

across the sands with Flora MacCambridge, his faithful nurse. But this same James Ranald, whose tombstone is in the Breckadale churchyard, grew up to confer reasonably with his ancient enemies and bring peace to the lands of Kintyre.'

'Remarkable,' commented the inspector. 'Reminds me of the yarns my father used to tell about Dunvegan in Skye.'

Dan brought the boat round inside the reef. On the port side, between them and the mouth of the Con, was a sheer sandstone cliff with a number of dark openings at its base.

Marlin threw his cigarette-end overboard, and as it sparked and disappeared quickly in the frothy wake he said, 'I think I see what you're getting at, Heathergill. Through it all there's a recurring theme – the victory of love over cruelty.'

'I'm glad you noticed that. It's the lesson of history, really, no matter what the pessimists say.'

'I wonder?'

Presently Dan eased back the motor and began to con the boat through a maze of seaweed-covered rocks. He pointed for'ard to the biggest of the openings in the cliff, now less than a hundred yards distant on the port bow. 'That's it,' he announced. 'That's Fingal's Cave.'

With skill based on a knowledge of almost every pebble on the Breckadale coastline, he edged the boat closer, eventually stopping her against a flat boulder to the left of the cave-mouth. Leaning out across the gun'le he secured the stern painter to a sharper rock beside it.

'You can go ashore here, gentlemen. Lucky the tide is out. You'll be able to reach the cave dry-shod, across the shingle.'

Hamish said, 'Aren't you coming with us?'

'Och, I'll just wait and look after the boat. Anyway, there's a wee maintenance job I want to do on the motor. . . . '

Hamish led MacLeod and Marlin across the shingle, avoiding the piles of glistening brown seaweed. They stopped at the entrance to the cave and looked up at a hundred feet of rugged sandstone soaring into the sky. Gulls wheeled and swooped, disturbed by the presence of humans.

'Difficult climb,' said Hamish.

'Ay. Even for giants twelve feet tall,' agreed the inspector.

Curiosity kindled in Marlin's hooded eyes. 'What's the idea? Are you suggesting someone climbed out of this cave to kill Finlay?'

'We're not suggesting it,' replied MacLeod. 'But some of the villagers are.'

Hamish said, 'Old Peggy McAllister thinks that on Saturday night she saw a man twelve feet tall at the scene of the murder. One of Fingal's smiths.'

They went inside, their footsteps on the sea-worn stones echoing in the roof. The acoustics made it obvious why at high tide, as the waves rushed in against the naked rock, a sound emerged like the metallic

118

thudding of hammers. Hamish was trying to explain this when, with a violent clapping of wings, a flock of pigeons erupted from the shadows and flew out into the daylight. The incident caused him a spasm of fear, but neither MacLeod nor Marlin seemed to be affected.

The cave was simply a hole in the ancient rock, a score of feet high and almost as many broad, created over millions of years by the thrusting tides.

The walls were rough and pitted, where quartzite pebbles had dropped out of the basic sandstone. A lower skirting of damp and slime, on which limpets and a delicate species of seaweed eked out a precarious existence, was displaced at a higher level by a bare, dry surface, in some of whose crevices grew tufts of ill-nourished sea-pinks.

The floor consisted mainly of shingle and small boulders smoothed and polished by constant rolling in the tidal drag. Across it, however, there ran a curious symmetrical vein of black whinstone, raised a few inches above the shingle and patterned by a series of small right-angled cracks.

MacLeod surveyed it, rubbing his chin. 'The anvil, eh?'

Hamish nodded. 'Stones lifted by the tide and hurled against it make a considerable noise.'

Marlin touched the rock with the sole of his shoe. 'Part of a dolerite dike,' he said.

The inspector's eyebrows went up. 'A what?'

'A dike. An intrusion in the old sediment marking the pipe of a volcanic eruption. This black stuff – dolerite –

is simply magna from the core of the earth, pressed and hardened. I did geology at the University,' Marlin went on to explain. 'And now I come to think of it, this particular dike is mentioned in the text-books. It runs across the Firth of Clyde, through the tip of Kintyre right up to the island of Mull.'

'Indeed,' said MacLeod, glancing briefly at the other with a hint of respect. 'We're always learning,' he added heavily.

They stepped on and over the whinstone slab. The cave grew darker as it narrowed and curved to the left. The atmosphere took on a musty odour, and their voices began to ring dully against the inward sloping rock.

Then the floor rose quickly, and almost without warning they reached the blank face of the inner wall. Hereabouts the shingle was dry, evidence that only on rare occasions did the sea penetrate as far. But Fingal's Cave had no other secrets to reveal.

Hamish had known that this would be the outcome; yet as he stood there, in the enclosed space, he had a slight bout of claustrophobia, aggravated by a feeling that invisible figures were looming gigantically in the half-light, watching and waiting. It appeared, however, that no such imaginative malaise troubled his companions.

After a time they made their way back to the entrance, shoes crunching and slithering on the smooth stones. The fresh, salty air had a pleasant tang after the smell of rotting seaweed and bird-droppings inside. Hamish, for one, breathed it in with relief.

Scrambling out to the flat rock where the boat was moored, they saw that Dan was fishing in the water with a boat-hook. As they stepped aboard he straightened up and disclosed his catch – a narrow strip of green webbing like the sling of an Army rifle.

'Och, we pick up a lot of things hereabouts,' he said. 'They're thrown into the burn and carried out to sea, but the way the tides are running they're soon dumped back among the rocks in here.'

MacLeod took the webbing and examined it. 'Hasn't been in the water long, eh?'

'Only a day or two by the look of it.'

'If someone dropped it in the burn on Saturday night, could the tides have brought it in already?'

'Ay. That's a very likely explanation, Inspector.'

Marlin said quickly, 'Couldn't it simply have fallen down the cliff?'

MacLeod glanced at Dan. 'What d'you think?'

'It's possible. It's certainly possible.' The old man turned away and began to tinker with the motor. Finally, without looking up, he added, 'You wouldn't be finding anything at all in the cave?'

'No blacksmiths or anvils, if that's what you mean,' replied the inspector, stuffing the webbing into his pocket. 'But it was an interesting trip. Very interesting indeed. . . . Care for a cigarette?'

'Och, many thanks. Stupid of me to have forgotten to fill my own case.' Dan lit up, started the motor, then settled himself at the tiller. 'If you please, Mr. Heathergill – the painter. . . .

'Ay, well,' he continued cheerfully, directing the boat towards the clearway beyond the reef, 'speaking about things falling down the cliff, did you ever hear the story of the big black bull that was grazing yonder at the bottom of Duncraig? He slipped and tumbled over into the sea, and because there was a high tide he didn't even hurt himself. Instead of making for the mouth of the burn, he began to swim right round the Rock – the way we're going ourselves at the moment – and reached the shore close to the jetty just as dawn was breaking. At that time Mr. Cattanach's place was still a lifeboat house, and Davie Read who used to be the caretaker – an old rascal, never sober and with about a dozen illegitimate children – Davie was shaving at the top window and saw this apparition emerging from the sea, all dripping and black. He thought it was the devil himself come to claim his own and made a beeline for the Manse, where he confessed his sins to the minister and signed the pledge. . . . Ay, it's great the things that happen in Breckadale, Inspector!'

MacLeod gave every sign of having enjoyed Dan's story. Even Marlin laughed. As for Hamish, he had been listening with only half an ear. His thoughts were entangled in a flimsy spider's web of fancy.

(3)

Marlin invited them all, including Dan, to share a pre-lunch drink with him at the hotel. Hamish took them in his car.

It was Sheena's morning off, and the bar was being

122

looked after by Patrick McConnachie. He greeted them with an affable smile which made up for the silence that fell awkwardly on a number of other guests clustered near the counter. MacLeod looked ordinary and comfortable – if a trifle formidable – in his flannels and sports jacket; but it was difficult to overlook the fact that he was hunting a killer and that as a result of the workings of his brain yet another killing might possibly take place on a scaffold.

Soon, however, the chatter became general again, Dan's booming voice providing a vital factor in the process. He was known to most of the visitors, and before long some of his most magnificent yarns were being given an airing.

In answer to a query from the inspector, Marlin said, 'I'm seeing Campbell this evening. He's coming down to dinner after his work. We may have some business to discuss, in connection with the future of the firm. As my partner's only surviving blood relation, he has an obvious interest, though a lot will depend on the provisions of Finlay's will.'

'McDermott was fairly wealthy, I gather?'

'Yes. The business has been doing well, and by the terms of our agreement he pocketed the lion's share of the profits.'

Hamish was surprised by a sharp edge in Marlin's voice, but MacLeod gave no sign of having noticed it. Calmly he went on, 'The widow will inherit most of the money, presumably?'

'Presumably. But I'm expecting a phone-call from his

123

lawyers this afternoon. They've promised to let me know the details.'

'I see.'

The topic was discarded in favour of listening to one of Dan's hair-raising stories. This one concerned a basking shark with which he had carried on a feud resembling that between Ahab and Moby Dick. In the end he had succeeded in harpooning it with a weapon forged in the Breckadale smithy; but the enormous sea-beast – 'fifty feet long if he was an inch' – had towed him 'half-way across the Atlantic' before finally admitting defeat.

The hotel gong sounding for lunch capped dramatically a highly dramatic tale.

8

Monday, 4.30 p.m. to 11 p.m.

(1)

MONDAY was to prove a time of decision for several people, including the murderer.

Sheena's decision was a simple one, containing no guile. That night, after the bar closed, she would hurry across the shore to Bruce's house. There she would beg his forgiveness and put aside the last traces of pride and prudery by offering to go in and, as he'd so often asked her to do, sit with him for a while and share his supper.

Acceptance of the idea quickly resolved the doubts that had troubled her during the week-end. From Inspector MacLeod she had learnt that Bruce loved and trusted her. Now it was her turn to prove that she loved and trusted him. She had come to understand how much she'd hurt him by her childishness. Now she would make up for it by giving herself to him without conditions. Even her body, if that would make him happy.

As she prepared in her bedroom for the evening spell of duty at the Breckadale Arms, her pulses were beating

125

with excitement. On the dressing-table her small transistor set – a present from Bruce – was softly playing a record by Alma Cogan: '*Love me tender, love me true. . . .*'

She chose her frock carefully, deciding at last on one with a flowered pattern and full skirt which Bruce had admired the last time they danced together. Before she put it on she looked at herself in the mirror, wondering if her body, when the time came, would prove exciting to Bruce. She thought also of his body – of the square chunkiness she'd so often seen clad only in bathing trunks – and for the first time allowed herself to imagine the feel of his nakedness against her own. She half expected the shame of the old wives' tales to overwhelm her at once, but instead there was only joy and a knowledge that Bruce's body would always be exciting to her.

Then she exchanged a smile with her reflection. What did bodies really matter? The warmth and completeness of love was the important thing. That was what both she and Bruce were needing, to give them courage.

'*Love me gladly, love me more. . . .*' Her head rustled up through thick folds of cotton. It was astonishing how free and secure she felt now that her mind was made up. Never before had she realized that an act of surrender could sometimes be a victory.

Gaily and acrobatically she zipped up the back of her frock. Then, as she brushed her hair, she made an effort to subdue the quickness of her breathing and persuade herself that for the time being at any rate she must act in a manner sensible and staid. Finally, experiencing an odd reluctance, she switched off the radio.

Before leaving she went to the back door and called through to the garden, 'I may be late tonight, Dad. Don't wait up for me.'

John McRae turned slowly on his sticks. 'That's all right, lass. Young Cattanach, eh?'

'Could be.'

'He's a lucky man.'

'I'm not so sure. Anyway, don't you stay out there too long and catch cold. Remember *Panorama*'s on at eight. Oh, and by the way, I've left your supper set, with some of your favourite sardine sandwiches.'

She blew him a kiss, and as she disappeared he smiled to himself with satisfaction. Whatever had been troubling her the previous night had evidently been forgotten. That was the way of youth, of course. Gay and sad and gay again.

It wasn't so simple when you were old and not much use to anybody. Then you had to cling stubbornly to an even humour, because if you didn't the game would be up.

(2)

When Sheena opened the cocktail bar her first customers were Colin Campbell and Marlin. Their moods were so obviously at variance that her attention was captured at once, even though Bruce remained steadily in her mind.

As Colin led the way in through the swinging glass

doors, he was bouncier than she had ever seen him. 'Okay, Peter,' he was saying, 'this is on me. Seems I can afford to buy you a drink at last.'

'Well, make it a small one.'

'Nonsense! Two doubles, Sheena.' He leant with his broad back to the counter and punched Marlin's shoulder. 'This is wonderful news,' he went on, 'and a complete surprise to me. Poor old Finlay! In my shoes he'd have been the very one to celebrate.'

The hood on the other's eyes failed to hide his edginess. 'In a way,' he said stiffly, 'I'm sorry for Alice.'

Proffering the whisky glasses, Sheena said, 'Plain water or ice, Colin?'

'Water for me. On the rocks for you, Peter?'

'Water will do. The alternative sounds almost like tempting Providence – in the circumstances.'

'Whatever you say. . . . Thanks, Sheena. We're having dinner later, so put it on my bill.'

'Yes, of course.'

The two men drank.

Colin lit a cigarette and exhaled luxuriously. 'What exactly did the lawyers say when they rang you up?'

'They gave me the bare facts. Nothing more. Alice will get her legal share – roughly a third. You get the rest.'

'They didn't mention how much?'

'No, but it's bound to be a hefty bit. So hefty, in fact, that if you decide to cash in on all of it, the future of McDermott & Marlin may be dicey – to say the least.'

'I see.' Colin grinned. 'That's why you were so keen I

should come and have dinner tonight – so that we could discuss business?'

Sheena was listening. She couldn't help herself. There was something impalpable between the two men – animosity, perhaps, cheerful on Colin's part, smouldering on Marlin's – and the overtones of their conversation fascinated her. Besides, the manner in which Marlin had spoken of McDermott's widow had stirred her romantically charged interest.

Another group of customers came in, and for a minute or two she was kept busy.

Then, as the newcomers drifted away from the counter, she heard Marlin say, 'I'll be quite frank. For Alice's sake – if not for mine – I'd be eternally grateful if you'd keep your money in the firm. Not all of it, maybe, but the greater part.'

'I'll have to think about that one,' said Colin lightly.

'It would be to your own benefit in the long run.' There was no lightness in Marlin's voice. 'We're doing well at the moment, and if we get this big hydro-electric contract you could easily double your money in five years.'

Colin shrugged. 'I'm like Finlay. I prefer my fun now – not when I'm too old to enjoy it.'

'I appreciate that. Believe me I do. But there's also Finlay's widow to think about—'

'Seems to me you're doing most of the thinking as far as she's concerned!'

Sheena had her back to them and appeared to be

absorbed in the polishing of a row of wine-glasses. In fact she was doing her best to catch every word, because from her point of view the conversation had now reached an intriguing climax. Was Marlin actually in love with McDermott's widow? She held her breath, so as not to miss his reply.

He cleared his throat, took another swallow of whisky and said with apparent calm, 'Again I'll be frank. As soon as decently possible, Alice and I intend to marry.'

Sheena gave a little sigh. Admiration crept into her mind for this big, rather ugly middle-aged man, who nevertheless was ready to champion the woman he loved in difficult circumstances and in face of considerable provocation from a younger and, as she now realized, a much less scrupulous man.

'So that's how the wind's been blowing!' Colin's laugh jarred on her. 'I might have known!'

'What do you mean by that?' said Marlin, his anger at last touching the limits of control.

'Nothing, nothing.' Colin laughed again, and put an arm about his shoulders. 'Simmer down, Peter. Remember you've got to stay friendly with me to get the money.'

If this is how sudden wealth affects your character, thought Sheena, let Bruce and me stay poor.

Slowly and grimly Marlin said, 'You remind me of Finlay – very forcibly. You're his cousin, all right!'

'Nobody,' replied Colin, unperturbed, 'has tried to murder *me*. Not yet. . . . Hey, Sheena!'

She started. 'Yes, Colin?'

'Set them up again, will you?'

'Certainly.'

As she poured out the whisky, he eyed her with cool appreciation. 'Say, that's a smart frock! Expecting your boy friend?'

'If you mean Bruce – no, I'm not. He has an article to write for the *Gazette*, so I expect he's working.'

'But you'll be calling on him later, eh?'

'Maybe.' The thought of being with Bruce in a few short hours made her smile back happily.

More people entered the bar. But a few minutes later, as he finished his second drink, she heard Colin say, 'After dinner I'll go home and think it all out, quietly and calmly.'

'Very well,' returned Marlin.

'And I'll give you my decision tomorrow. After the funeral, before you and Alice leave for Glasgow. How's that?'

'Fine, Colin.' They began to move towards the swing doors. 'But don't rush it. There's plenty of time. All the time in the world.'

(3)

Janet's day had been less nerve-racking than the previous one, though the phone still rang occasionally as various reporters tried to contact Inspector Mac-Leod. Following lunch he had retired to the study to confer with various police messengers from Kinloch, and her afternoon had been spent in comparative peace.

She had picked some gooseberries in the garden and made a pot or two of jam.

Hamish had visited the kitchen several times, ostensibly to see how the jam was getting on, but in fact to find relief in her company while he waited nervously for something to happen.

She had tried to soothe him by initiating a calm survey of events. 'Darling, you've written twenty-nine detective stories. Your detective works out each problem with unfailing logic. Can't you do the same with this one?'

He had sat on the edge of the sink, looking miserable. 'It's easy to work out a thing logically when you plant the clues yourself! This is different. I can't even spot what the real clues are.'

'Won't the inspector tell you?'

'No fear! And d'you know why? I'm one of his suspects.'

'Oh, nonsense!'

'I'm telling you! It – it's a great strain, Janet.'

'But you're always saying in your books that motive is the important thing. What possible motive could you have for killing McDermott?'

'Duncan may be trying to find one.'

'He did ask me what you were doing between half-past ten and eleven o'clock on Saturday night. But he accepted what I told him – that we were in the study having a cup of tea and that you were lecturing me on the plot of your next detective story.'

'I'll never have the nerve to write another detective

story after this! In any case, a wife's testimony is no good in a court of law.'

'Oh, Hamish, for heaven's sake!'

He had suddenly laughed and, jumping down from his perch on the sink, had begun to waltz her round, endangering the bubbling jelly-pan on the cooker. 'Sorry – I'm being a bore,' he had said. 'But d'you know what? An hour ago my publisher rang up to tell me that the new book's beginning to sell like hot cakes, thanks to the publicity in the *Clarion*.'

She had stopped his gyrations by tweaking his ear. Up like a sputnik, down like a spent meteor. That was Hamish Heathergill. He certainly wasn't the solidest and most phlegmatic husband in the world. But then, she'd have disliked it if he was.

She'd kissed him and sent him out to rake the gravel on the driveway.

Now, as she cleared away the tea-things, staunchly refusing to allow him and the inspector to do the washing-up again, she was glad to notice that his mood had become less excitable.

The reason, she deduced, lay in a piece of advice that MacLeod had given him. 'Go ahead. Telephone your article to the paper as it stands. I'm fairly certain there won't be an arrest tonight.'

When Janet finally left the room, however, Hamish looked squarely at his friend and said, 'Why won't there be an arrest tonight?'

The inspector looked down at the tip of his cigarette. 'Certain technical tests have to be made.

I shan't know the results until tomorrow morning.'

'That's all you're prepared to say?'

'That's all.'

'Even to an official correspondent of the *Clarion*?'

'Even to the great Hamish Heathergill.'

'I see. All right, Duncan. But—'

'When the time comes, you'll get your exclusive. I give you my word.'

(4)

The time was then seven o'clock. At half-past there was a phone call to say that Sergeant MacPherson was waiting to see the inspector at the hotel.

Soon after MacLeod's departure Hamish rang the *Clarion* office and dictated his article to a copy-typist. Thereafter he pottered about in the garden, trying to do odd jobs.

As twilight was beginning to fall, Janet found him in the vegetable plot absent-mindedly uprooting her young lettuce-plants. His excuse was that he'd mistaken them for weeds, and his contrition was so patent that she couldn't bring herself to be angry with him.

'Look,' she said, 'why don't you go across and see Bruce?'

'He – he's probably working. The review for the *Gazette*.'

'He ought to have finished that by now. In any case I'm becoming a wee bit worried. Nobody's seen him all day. It may be that he's working hard, but I've a feeling there's something else. D'you think he's had a quarrel with Sheena?'

'What about?'

'All those tales going around. You know, McDermott having her photo in his pocket . . .'

'A lot of damned rubbish!'

' 'A lot of damned rubbish my foot! Of course, it's ridiculous to say that Sheena was philandering with McDermott, but though *you* may not believe it, some men can be extraordinarily jealous.'

'So what?'

'Oh, never mind! The fact remains that Bruce appears to have gone into hiding. Something's on his mind – and you may be able to help him.'

'H'm. You could be right.'

'Anyway, it'll give you an object in life. You've been mooning around all day like a displaced person.'

'What about you? Alone in the bungalow, I mean.'

'Be your age, darling! I'm accustomed to being alone.'

'Well – I *will* go and see him. I've been worrying about him, too.'

'I know. The trouble is, you've been afraid he may have something unpleasant to tell you.'

'Yes.'

'Knowing Bruce, I think you're utterly mistaken. . . . Now, off you go. I'll have a cup of tea ready when you come back.'

He put on a windcheater over his cardigan and set out along the shore. The dusk was quiet, and on his short journey he encountered only a few stragglers from the caravans: a young couple dreamily holding hands and a father herding his small twin sons to bed.

As he approached the house a light went on in the front window, evidence that Bruce was at home. This at any rate, was a relief.

He knocked and heard an irritable shout, 'Who's there?'

He went in.

Bruce was at the table, hunched over his typewriter. Sheets of paper – some virgin, some irreparably crumpled – lay scattered on the table and on the floor. He had on his thick, dark blue guernsey. His hair was uncombed, his chin unshaven and black.

Overcoming a spasm of nervous embarrassment, Hamish said, 'Sorry! I didn't know you were working. If I'm being a damned nuisance . . .'

Bruce got up, his smile betraying both relief and pleasure. 'You're never a nuisance, man! Sit down.' As his visitor obeyed, he took up a stance at the fireplace and went on, 'As a matter of fact I was just thinking of going across and having a word with yourself and Janet. It's been bloody awful, here alone. Look, what about a drink?'

'Well – if there's any whisky . . .'

'Sure. I still have some of the Islay Mist you gave me at Christmas.'

He hurried to the kitchen and came back with a bottle and tumblers. He poured out two stiff ones.

Having savoured his first mouthful, Hamish said, 'I slipped out for a breath of air and saw your light.

Between you and me,' he continued, stretching an elastic conscience still further, 'Janet's being a bit temperamental. You know, the inspector around all day, people in and out . . .'

'I don't blame her. It's a hell of an imposition.'

'I know. My fault, too. I thought it was a chance to study real detection.'

'Women don't look at things the way we do.'

'You're telling me! And as it turns out, I've learnt more about detection from a page of Agatha Christie than I have from Duncan all week-end! But never mind that. What are you writing?'

'My piece for the *Gazette*. Just about finished, thank God! I'll post it in the morning.'

'Well done! The first in a series is always the most difficult.'

Bruce took a gulp from his tumbler, careless of the fact that Islay Mist should be sipped slowly, like brandy. 'It's not easy writing anything these days, with your girl's good name being dirtied about by policemen – and by all those clots in the caravans!'

Though conscious of the need to tread warily, Hamish found himself saying, 'Your own good name is under suspicion.'

'Mine doesn't matter. But I'll tell you one thing – I didn't murder Finlay McDermott, though I'd like to have done it!'

'I see. Get it off your chest, Bruce.'

'All right.' He strode across and sat on a corner of the table. 'As far as I can make out, they're trying to insinuate that Sheena had fallen for him, just as he fell for her. It's a damned lie!'

'I know.'

'That photo in his pocket. She was showing it to McConnachie in the bar on Saturday evening. McDermott snatched it out of her hand. *She* didn't tell me. McConnachie did. A decent bloke. He came here to the house last night, of his own accord.'

Bruce gulped down more whisky. Hamish said nothing, aware that unrestricted talk has considerable therapeutic value.

'The trouble is, I get so fiendishly jealous. I suppose Sheena was afraid to tell me about it herself in case I'd fly off the handle again. Maybe I should have gone to see her tonight at the hotel, but there was this job, and – and anyway, after the row we had on Saturday night she may never want to set eyes on me again! This row, Hamish – it happened without warning, like an earthquake. I accused her of being too friendly with McDermott. No wonder she was wild. When I think about it – reasonably – I can understand that she *had* to put up with him. She has her invalid father – and she can't afford to lose her job. But when we're together, and – and . . .'

His swift, slightly incoherent words trailed to a stop.

Hamish said, 'You do mean to marry her?'

'Yes, yes, yes! If she'll have me. If I can save some money. And I should be able to save some money, with the *Gazette* contract. People say it won't work out.

She says it herself at times. But I'm not all that difficult to live with, am I?'

'Of course not,' replied Hamish, with a few mental reservations.

'As for Sheena,' Bruce went on, 'she's beautiful, she's innocent. In her heart she's far more of a poet than I'll ever be—'

He broke off. An unexpected sound had suddenly come from outside, in the direction of the jetty.

(5)

Though the cocktail bar had closed at the usual time, various odd jobs kept Sheena busy until half-past ten. A few minutes later she said goodnight to Patrick Mc-Connachie, who generally remained on duty until after midnight.

He smiled at her. 'Man, you're looking great tonight! If I was twenty years younger, Bruce Cattanach wouldn't be having it all his own way, I can tell you!'

'Listen to him! The most eligible bachelor in Brecka-dale coming the old man stuff!'

He chuckled, looking after her with affection.

As she went out through the hall Inspector MacLeod and Sergeant MacPherson were sitting in a corner, deep in talk; but they looked up and returned her friendly wave.

The night air was chilly. She put on her coat, thrusting her hands deep in the pockets. As she walked lightly and quickly down the steep road to the shore, it flared and flaunted open.

139

She met no one in the dark. When she reached the stile leading on to the shore it was almost wholly quiet, except for the murmer of the sea. Then she heard the sound of a car crossing the golf course and stopping near the caravans. Holidaymakers, she thought, returning from an evening in Kinloch.

The beach was littered with small piles of drying seaweed, but though there was no moon she could still see and avoid them.

Her high heels sank in the sand, and several times she almost lost a shoe, but such small inconveniences had no effect on her good spirits. Already she could see Duncraig ahead of her, a huge shadow against the indigo sky, and under Duncraig was Bruce's house, with a light shining in the front window.

This was going to be the happiest night of her life. She knew it. No longer was she troubled by a sense of inferiority. Recognizing and surrendering to her own love for Bruce, she had become certain of his love for her. Not for a moment did she imagine that he might be unhappy to see her. When he opened that door he was going to be thrilled as she was now.

Sandpipers rose up, squawking. She gave a little start and then laughed at her fears. As the beating of her heart became steadier she breathed in the salty air with pleasure.

Encountering a patch of slippery shingle, she danced lightly across it, giving her feet no time to sink. She went dancing on for a yard or two more, singing to herself a song of Adam Faith's.

Suddenly a solitary boulder loomed up among the sand. Here, according to the story, was where Flora MacCambridge, escaping from besieged Duncraig with the infant James Ranald MacDonald in her arms, had been challenged by a Campbell sentry.

'Who are you?' he had asked, in the Gaelic.

'The wife of one of your soldiers. My baby is teething – and fretful. I am trying to put him to sleep.'

In the moonlight the man had peered at the plaid-swathed bundle. He'd said, 'The tartan about him may be Campbell, but his eyes – blue and dark as the island seas – his eyes are the eyes of a MacDonald.' She had begun to deny it, but with a smile he'd silenced her. 'I have no quarrel with children, my dear. Go your way, and the blessing of Columba be with you.'

Like most other Breckadale youngsters, Sheena had been told the story of Flora the faithful nurse, in her early days at school; but it had been Bruce, one evening as they sat together on this rock, who had made it vivid and memorable for her. Afterwards she had said, 'The way you tell it would appeal to children. Why don't you make it into a radio play?'

He'd frowned for a minute. Then he'd answered, 'Darling, that's an idea.'

The script had eventually been broadcast as a programme for Scottish children. Later it had been repeated in all the Regions, and a number of critics had taken time off from praising *Z Cars* to be highly complimentary about it. He had used part of his fee to buy her the transistor; but though his present made her

141

happy, the thought that she'd been able to help and encourage him made her happier still.

She had suggested subjects for other radio programmes. One, based on the legend of Columba's coming to Breckadale, had already been written and paid for by the BBC. Another – about the seals which came up on the rocks on a winter's morning, looking like great prehistoric birds as they arched their backs – was in process of being written.

She went on past the rock, singing again. But this time it was a Highland cradle-song that had been a recurring theme in the production of Bruce's play.

The light in the window came nearer. Instead of embarking on a long detour through the dunes, she decided to take a short cut to the house by way of the tidal rocks near the jetty. With her high heels this may have been a wrong decision, but she had often used the short cut before and knew the easiest way.

As she crossed the pebble-laden sandstone, testing seaweed-filled hollows with the toes of her shoes, an indefinite sound occurred on the beach to her left, as if something had moved heavily but quickly in the soft sand. She saw nothing, however, and concluded that it had been a piece of turf slipping down from the dunes. This sometimes happened after children had spent the day digging sand out of the wrong places.

But now her happy mood was tinged with uneasiness. The darkness that had been kind before seemed to have acquired a quality of menace. She began to hurry. One heel stuck in a small fissure and she overbalanced and fell on all-fours. In a flurry of near-panic she jerked her heel clear.

She stood up, brushing damp lichen-marks from the skirts of her coat and frock, and even in the midst of her inexplicable fear was annoyed to discover that one of her nylons had been slightly torn.

Something moved behind her. She half-turned and saw a towering figure.

Terror paralysed her muscles. Her brain registered a gigantic male, though the features, under the down-turned brim of a soft hat, were unrecognizable in the dark.

The man swung a weapon high in the air – it might have been a club, a bar of steel, a wooden pole – she couldn't be sure. It came hurtling down towards her head, momentarily flashing in the meagre light reflected from a rock-pool.

She regained her voice and power of movement and screamed and flung herself down and to one side. A jagged edge of rock bruised her hip, but she scarcely felt the pain. The weapon struck a vein of quartz inches from her face, and sparks showered up.

The man heaved himself upright, again whirling the weapon high. She screamed again and scrambled desperately, like a wounded animal, further to the right. A button of her coat caught in a crevice, but in a nightmare moment she pulled and tore it off. The weapon came sweeping down. As she swung clear and rolled over a ledge, there was another crash and a hail of sparks.

Scrabbling and screaming, she fell into a shallow pool. Cold water clutched her body, threatening to choke her. Above, outlined against the sky, her enemy stood poised, preparing, as she thought, to leap down on her.

But as she gasped and tried to scream again, the door of Bruce's house, less than fifty yards away, was flung open. She heard his urgent voice, 'We're coming, Sheena! We're coming!'

The man on the ledge moved quickly and was suddenly gone.

She splashed up and on to the rocks. She had lost one of her shoes, but that didn't matter. Bruce was there – and Mr. Heathergill behind him.

She ran, hobbling, into his arms, and he caught her close. He felt her trembling like a small and frightened bird. He heard her sobbing, 'Bruce! Oh, Bruce! He tried to kill me!'

He stroked her hair. 'You're safe now. You're safe.'

Hamish stood awkwardly beside them. 'It's all over,' he said, trying to sound comforting. 'There's nothing to be afraid of. . . . Listen, Bruce. I'm going back in to phone Duncan at the hotel. He must be told about this.'

'You do that. We'll be with you in a minute.'

When they were alone, Sheena whispered, 'Bruce, I was coming to see you. To – to be with you in your house as you wanted. Then all of a sudden, in the dark, it happened.'

Up on the golf course an engine was started, and a car went whining away.

He said, 'Who was it?'

'I don't know. He came behind me. . . . I – I'm sorry, darling. I mean about Saturday night. I'll make it up to you.'

'Don't worry.' His voice was unsteady, but gentle, too. 'I was to blame. I was jealous. I was jealous because – because I love you.'

'Oh, Bruce, I love you, too. I need you.'

She clung to him as if she never meant to let him go.

9

Monday 11 p.m. and onwards.

(1)

WHEN Sergeant MacPherson set out for Kinloch at about a quarter to eleven, Inspector MacLeod was left alone in the hall of the hotel, except for occasional guests passing upstairs from the main lounge to the second floor.

All his plans were laid, all his instructions given. In the morning he would receive answers to three technical questions, and if these were in the affirmative, as he expected, then the evidence against the murderer would be solider than a stone wall and an arrest could be made at once. He had plenty of indirect evidence already, of course, but he needed the facts – the technical facts – to satisfy the Procurator Fiscal.

He was conscious of having done a reasonably sound and speedy professional job. It wasn't often the Argyll Police were faced with a murder, but when they were – well, he was happy to think that in this case no outside help had been requested or required.

Patrick McConnachie approached with a glass and

146

a small bottle on a tray. 'Your nightcap, sir. Scotch and ginger ale.'

'Oh, thanks. Good thing Mr. Heathergill isn't here to condemn the ginger ale!'

'Ay. Plain water or nothing for Mr. Heathergill. "Uncivilized" – that's his opinion of anything else in whisky.'

'Every man to his taste, McConnachie.'

'That's right, sir. All them "connosoors" – they do a bit of posing at times. Will you be wanting an early call in the morning?'

'It depends.' MacLeod drank with appreciation. 'By the way,' he said, 'I don't see Mr. Marlin about.'

'He went off in his car. Soon after they'd had dinner and Mr. Campbell left for Kinloch. He hasn't come in yet.'

'Did he mention where he was going?'

'Not to me, sir. But he did say . . . well, I heard him muttering about the hotel being full of damned police-men and that he wanted a breath of decent air.'

'I see. I didn't realize that Sergeant MacPherson and I were upsetting your guests.'

'Och, the rest of them are not at all upset. The very opposite. It gives them plenty to talk about.' McCon-nachie frowned. Suddenly, glancing round almost furtively, he cleared his throat and said, 'Between ourselves, sir, I've been wondering what's come over Mr. Marlin. All this evening he's been different – narkier somehow: not nearly so cool and calm as he was. Before he went out, for instance – about an hour ago –

he was making an awful row about his club. You know, the one Colin Campbell brought back yesterday.'

'Was he, indeed?'

'Ay. It's disappeared out of his bag again – or so he says. The way he was going on you'd think it was my fault! And the truth is, I wouldn't know a 9-iron from – from one of Fingal's hammers!'

'Neither would old Peggy, I imagine.'

MacLeod poured the last of the ginger ale into his glass, and there was a silence while McConnachie digested this unexpected rejoinder.

At last, curiosity proving stronger than his awe of authority, he lowered his voice and said, 'If it's not an impertinent question, sir, have you come to any conclusion yet?'

MacLeod considered. A small seed planted in the right place might bear unexpected fruit. Besides, he liked McConnachie and found pleasure in the idea of giving him a vicarious thrill.

At last he said, 'If you mean do I know who the murderer is, the answer is yes.'

'Merciful goodness! Is that a fact?'

'Our case is almost complete. In the meantime, of course, we're keeping the person's identity to ourselves—'

The telephone rang.

McConnachie jerked upright like a startled colt. 'Oh – er – excuse me, sir,' he stammered, putting down the tray and almost running towards one of the call-boxes.

He came back, eyes wide with further sensation. 'It's

148

Mr. Heathergill, sir. Phoning from Mr. Cattanach's place. There's been an accident.'

'What!'

'They're wanting you over there as soon as possible.'

'Did he say what kind of accident?'

'No, sir, he didn't. I was wondering—'

'Right.' MacLeod got up, swallowing the last of his whisky and cutting speculation short. 'By the way, if anyone rings me here before I get back, tell them to try Mr. Cattanach's number.'

'I'll do that, sir. I'll certainly do that. Will you be taking your own car?'

'Ay. Otherwise I might get lost on a dark night like this!'

(2)

'. . . and so I took the short cut over the rocks, Inspector. He came from behind. He had some kind of weapon that – that glinted even in the dark. Oh, it was horrible!'

'I understand how you feel, Miss McRae.' Seated opposite her at Bruce's work-table, MacLeod's voice was sympathetic.

From the fireplace, where he stood listening with Hamish, Bruce said, quietly, 'Go on, darling. Tell him everything.'

Momentarily she glanced across, with a small smile of thanks for his encouragement. She still looked pale and shivery, though her wet clothes had been discarded and she now wore a suit of his pyjamas under a thick, padded dressing-gown.

'He – he struck at me,' she explained, turning again to the inspector and fumbling with her handkerchief, 'but I threw myself down and to the side and – and he missed. The weapon struck the rocks beside me, and sparks flew up. He tried to strike me again, but I scrambled back and fell over a ledge into a pool. Then – then Bruce saved my life, because when he started shouting the man ran away.'

'He had a car,' Hamish put in. 'On the golf course. A minute or two later I heard him drive off.'

'H'm. But of course, you don't know for certain it was *his* car?'

'Well, I suppose not. It's a fair inference, though.'

MacLeod made no comment.

To Sheena he said, 'Did you notice anything distinctive about him? Was he right- or left-handed, for instance?'

She shook her head. 'I – I was frightened. I didn't really see him very well.'

'How could she!' demanded Bruce. 'The attack was so sudden, so unexpected—'

'I know, I know!' The interruption came irritably. MacLeod continued, 'Miss McRae, I have to ask you certain questions – not because I want to snoop into your private affairs but because the answers you give may lead me to your attacker.' Unexpectedly he smiled at her across the table, and Hamish was delighted to notice his evident affection and regard.

'I understand,' said Sheena.

'Good. Now tell me, had you any particular reason for coming to visit Mr. Cattanach – so late?'

She stretched her handkerchief between her hands, tugging it taut. She liked the inspector. After their talk the previous day, his image in her mind was that of a father figure, strict as to duty but gentle-hearted in personal relationships. Solidly sympathetic though he might be, however, she found it impossible to reply with complete frankness. Were she to do so, it would cause everyone embarrassment. After a moment's thought, therefore, she decided to uncover only a minor part of the truth.

She said: 'I – I wanted to tell Bruce what happened this evening, in the hotel. It's not really important, but . . .'

'Go on, Miss McRae.'

She glanced at Bruce, who smiled and nodded. Hamish froze into an attitude of keen attention.

'Well,' she said, slowly. 'Mr. Marlin had Colin Campbell down for a drink and a meal. Before dinner they were in the bar. I heard them discussing business. I think Mr. Marlin was suggesting that Colin should become a partner in the firm, now that his cousin is dead. Then Mr. Marlin said that – that as soon as decently possible he intends to marry Alice, Finlay McDermott's widow.'

'I see.' Leaning forward against the edge of the table, MacLeod remained motionless, but his expression had suddenly been replaced by one that was blank and

151

official. 'I see,' he repeated. 'You thought this would interest Mr. Cattanach?'

'Oh, I know it sounds silly. But I was so surprised—'

'Sounds silly nothing!' Bruce rapped out. 'She's a woman, Inspector. It's a piece of red-hot gossip, and gossip is important – especially to a woman. Why shouldn't she want to share it?'

'Exactly,' said Hamish, admiring not only Bruce's warm defence of his girl but also his quickness in calling psychology to his aid.

Impassively, MacLeod inclined his head. 'Quite so. I agree. But there's another consideration. Miss McRae, can you suggest a possible reason for the attack?'

She hesitated. Finally she answered, 'No, I can't. I'm sorry.'

'Please think.' He regarded her steadily. 'There may be something that you don't realize is important.'

But she kept tugging at her handkerchief, without inspiration. 'I can't think of anything. Honestly.'

MacLeod sighed. Then he sat back in his chair, allowing himself a faint smile. 'Ay, well, it seems our murderer is inclined to be conservative,' he said. 'In his choice of weapon, I mean. However—'

The telephone on the desk began to ring. Like a greyhound from a trap Bruce leapt towards it.

After a moment he said, 'For you, Inspector. Sergeant MacPherson from Kinloch.'

As MacLeod listened, his heavy face was again drained of expression, though when he replaced the receiver and returned to stand against one end of the table, anger showed in his eyes.

'Colin Campbell reports that he also has been the victim of an attack. In Kinloch. It seems that about five minutes ago he was returning to his hotel – after posting letters – when a man leapt out at him from a dark entrance. He got a nasty blow above his left eye, but when he started shouting for help the man disappeared. He's at the police station now, receiving first aid.'

'He's not badly hurt then?' said Hamish.

'According to MacPherson, just a small cut and bruising. But he finds it impossible to identify or even to describe his assailant – except that he was tall and wore a soft hat. I don't blame him. The thing must have happened very quickly.'

Bruce said: 'Could it have been the same man who went for Sheena?'

'Ay – if he had a car, as Hamish suggested.' He consulted his wrist-watch. 'It's now more than half-an-hour since Miss McRae saw him.'

'Duncan,' exclaimed Hamish, 'what in the world does all this mean?'

MacLeod looked him straight in the eye. 'It means, I think, that somebody is losing his nerve.'

There was a slightly awkward silence, broken at last by Bruce. 'What's going to happen to Sheena?' he said. 'I mean, the murderer tried to kill her once. He may try to kill her again. She can't be left alone all night with only her father to protect her.'

'I see your point.' Lifting one eyebrow, MacLeod continued, 'Hamish, could you and your wife give Miss McRae a bed?'

'Yes, certainly. But—'

'I'll put a policeman on. The most efficient I can spare.' Noticing concern in Sheena's eyes, he added, quickly, 'And another on your father's place. That will be adequate, in the circumstances.'

It appeared that the matter had been finally settled when all at once Bruce struck the mantelpiece with his fist and exclaimed, 'Look, you're not going to keep *me* out of this! We're practically engaged, and if Sheena's in any danger—'

'There's a simple solution,' said Hamish, gallantly ignoring a niggling fear of Janet's wrath. 'You come along and stay with us as well.'

'But – but what about—'

'We'll share the spare bedroom, you and I. Sheena can sleep with Janet. All right, Duncan?'

'Ay, just the thing. Couldn't be better.'

Bruce remained dour and unsettled, but he smiled crookedly and said, 'Thanks, Hamish. Thanks once again.' Then he went across and took Sheena's hand. 'You'll be safe now,' he told her. 'You're not to worry any more.'

She smiled up at him, the bright cloud of her hair resting against the rough, dark blue sleeve of his guernsey.

'Well, hadn't we better be moving?' said the inspector.

Hamish nodded. 'I'll go straight home across the beach and – er – let Janet know. You bring Sheena, Bruce, after you tell her father what's going on. You'll give them a lift in your car, won't you, Duncan?'

'Of course. A pleasure.'

'Right,' said Bruce. 'Come on, darling. Better collect your things.'

She got up. 'Inspector, are you – are you quite sure Dad will come to no harm?'

'He'll be safe until tomorrow, Miss McRae. That I promise. And tomorrow it will all be over.'

(3)

Hamish was shocked and puzzled by the shape of events. As he gangled swiftly across the dark beach, however, he was equally concerned about what Janet's reaction might be to the prospect of entertaining two unexpected guests.

In one way or another he was so upset that he blundered straight into the sitting-room and, finding his wife comfortably reading a magazine, made a bald and unprefaced announcement.

'Janet, Sheena and Bruce are coming to stay the night.'

She put down the magazine and got slowly to her feet. 'What's that you're saying?'

'Sheena and Bruce. They're coming to stay. Somebody tried to murder Sheena. And Colin Campbell.'

'Take a seat, Hamish. You look feverish. Now, calmly and soberly, tell me what all this is about.'

When he had recounted the facts, he was surprised by the change in her attitude. There was no resentment, no complaints about his impulsive offer of hospitality. In fact, being full of sympathy for Sheena and Bruce, she complimented him on it. Considerably relieved, he was happy to take part in the swift organization of tea and sandwiches, hot-water bottles for the spare bedroom beds and the transference of some of his own effects from one bedroom to the other.

'I knew it,' he kept muttering, padding back and forth at her heels. 'I knew you'd turn up trumps!'

'It's the least we can do. Poor Sheena! What a terrible experience!'

'Duncan is convinced that she knows something. Something she's seen or heard, which the murderer has realized may incriminate him. But so far she hasn't been able to think what it can be.'

'Look, go and switch on the electric blankets in the beds in our room. Lucky you never sleep in the one you're supposed to sleep in! No need to change the sheets.'

MacLeod came in with the young ones, and they ate and drank together. At first, both Sheena and Bruce were inclined to be quiet, Bruce in particular having a silent edginess about him that caused Hamish some misgiving. But under the influence of Janet's chatter and the inspector's solid calm – not to mention a hilarious story told by Hamish about Dan the

Dooker – they presently began to behave more naturally and to show an unaffected happiness in being together.

The inspector left about one o'clock. Sheena insisted on helping Janet to clear up, while Hamish, carefully avoiding the subject of the murder, discussed with Bruce a literary controversy currently being aired in the London reviews.

Later, when they went to bed, the discussion was continued. Hamish felt sleepy, but in the next bed Bruce kept up a spate of talk. Outside it was quiet, except for the pulse of the sea, though at one point they heard a car stopping not far from the front gate. A police car, by the sound of its engine.

About three o'clock Hamish was dropping off when Bruce turned restlessly and said, 'Why were you and MacLeod so determined to bring Sheena here? Couldn't you have trusted me to look after her in her own home? Or in *my* home, for that matter!'

Hamish sighed. 'It's not a question of trust. Duncan and I are old squares. We were thinking of the proprieties.'

'The proprieties? Good grief! At this time of day!'

'The time of night has more relevance,' returned Hamish, with unaccustomed sharpness. 'You're part of a community here. You don't want to begin your life with Sheena on the wrong foot. For Sheena's sake. That's all there is to it. Now, do me a favour and go to sleep. I need my five hours if you don't!'

Suddenly Bruce laughed. 'All right, Hamish. Or should I say, "old pop"?'

'Huh! Don't kid yourself. When I'm eighty you'll be sixty, and there won't be so damned much difference!'

10

(1)

NEXT morning Sheena and Bruce were in good spirits, apparently enjoying the flavour of domesticity as they breakfasted with their hosts. Janet, too, whatever her private thoughts may have been, gave every sign of happy unconcern.

Hamish's mood was different. As the others chatted over extra cigarettes and cups of coffee, he wandered out on to the lawn, painfully conscious of increasing tension.

He saw the blue water of the bay, with the image of Duncraig reflected across it. He saw the holidaymakers busy about the caravans, children already invading the beach. He saw a liner in the distance, passing out through the North Channel to the Atlantic, its white superstructure glistening in the sun. He saw farmers' tractors and trailers darting about in the hayfields like beetles.

More particularly he saw a police car, parked in a lay-by along the road. Inside it was a uniformed

159

constable, watching and waiting. But Hamish knew that the time of waiting was almost at an end. Before the day was out he would write a final article for the *Clarion* which would almost certainly contain the name of the murderer. The thought tended to make him physically sick.

But it was curious how life and the little preoccupations of life went on, in spite of the ugliness behind it. As he re-entered the house he heard Janet and Sheena laughing their heads off at some satirical verses Bruce had just made up about the Secretary of State for Scotland – a publicity-prone individual who loudly demanded more grants and subsidies for his numerous farming constituents, but refused, with righteous indignation, to support the idea that authors and publishers, despite their low voting power, should be entitled to a tiny royalty on books borrowed free from a public library.

At the front door Hamish glanced back at Duncraig. This time, behind and beyond it, he saw clouds heaving up over the horizon and realized that the spell of fine weather might soon be coming to an end. In fact, a slow swell was already oiling into the bay, promising a rising wind from the south.

(2)

At about the same time, while smoking an after-breakfast cigarette in the lounge of the hotel, MacLeod was approached by Peter Marlin. They exchanged watchful nods.

Marlin said, 'You are probably wondering where I was last night?'

'Curiosity is one of my strongest characteristics,' agreed the inspector.

'The truth is, I was browned off. I got into my car and drove all the way round Kintyre – a distance on the clock of about a hundred miles.'

'Indeed,' said MacLeod.

'Actually I didn't return until after midnight and was therefore unpopular with Patrick McConnachie.'

'Feeling better this morning?'

'Well – Finlay's widow is coming today. After the funeral in Kinloch she and I are driving back to Glasgow. Something to look forward to.'

'I've no doubt you'll be glad to leave all this unpleasantness behind. The funeral service is in the hospital chapel, I believe?'

'Yes. Thereafter from the mortuary to the town cemetery. Colin tells me the family have a private lair.'

The inspector kept his back to the light from the window. 'I hear that Mrs. McDermott gets no more than her legal share of her husband's estate?'

'Quite right,' said Marlin, putting his lighter to a cigarette with his left hand. 'When they separated, Finlay made a new will, leaving the residue to his cousin.'

'Was she disappointed?'

'Not unduly so.'

'Mr. Campbell would be surprised by his good luck?'

'Very surprised, though naturally delighted, too. I

have been trying to persuade him to keep his money in the business. If he decides not to, I'm afraid Alice and I will be hard pressed to keep the firm going.'

'Has anyone told you that Mr. Campbell was attacked last night?'

'What!'

'It seems that after he left you here he went straight home and wrote a few letters. On the way back after posting them, he was set upon by someone he couldn't identify – a tall man with a soft hat.'

'Was he – was he badly injured?'

'No. As soon as he began shouting for help the man ran off. Miss McRae was attacked, too, you know – about half-an-hour earlier. On the tidal rocks near Bruce Cattanach's place.'

'By the same man?'

'Presumably.'

'Good heavens! What's going on, Inspector?'

'I have a fair idea. Though a few pieces of the puzzle are still missing.'

McConnachie came in, eyes conspiratorial. 'Inspector,' he said, almost in a whisper. 'Sergeant MacPherson has arrived and is wanting to see you as soon as possible.'

'Thanks. I'll be with him right away.'

(3)

Leaving Sergeant MacPherson in the car outside, MacLeod called at Hamish's bungalow shortly before mid-day.

Hamish met him at the door. 'Duncan, Sheena thinks she may have remembered something that could account for the attempt on her life.'

'Well now, isn't that remarkable! But look, has she—'

'She hasn't told any of us. Says it's too far-fetched. But I persuaded her you'd be interested just the same.'

'Good. May I see her alone?'

'Of course. But mind your step. Bruce is guarding her like a suspicious watch-dog!'

'Poets are not in my line as a rule, but this Bruce Cattanach has given me an entirely new interest in the species. . . . Incidentally, Sergeant MacPherson and I are on our way down to the burn at the seventeenth green. Mr. Marlin will be joining us; and since Colin Campbell has the day off for the funeral – and seems quite fit after his nasty experience last night – I have arranged that he should be there, too. I think you and your growling poet should tag along.'

Hamish sighed. 'Grandstand finish, Duncan?'

'Something like that. I promised you an exclusive. Remember?'

(4)

The policemen had gone. Hamish and Bruce had gone.

The sky was clouding over. A chill wind was blowing, ruffling the sea and threatening rain. In the distance the Hammers of Fingal had begun to beat.

Janet and Sheena were in the sitting-room cleaning spoons.

'When I'm worried,' said Janet, 'when I'm faced with a crisis I can't do anything about, I always clean the spoons. I find it remarkably soothing.'

Sheena said, 'I don't know how to thank you. You and Mr. Heathergill have been wonderful to us.'

'You put on the Silvaclean. I'll do the polishing.'

'Yes, all right.' After a moment Sheena continued, 'How on earth have you coped with it all? The inspector for almost every meal. People in and out, drinking coffee. Then us, last night.'

'I like having you and Bruce. But I could have strangled Hamish for becoming involved with the inspector!'

'He's sweet – Mr. Heathergill, I mean. Bruce thinks the world of him.'

'I do, too, I suppose. But you know, marrying a writer – it's absolute hell at times. You'll find out.'

'But surely—'

'Oh, I know. There are compensations. When they're so inclined they love us like angels. But when they're working – making magic with words or thinking out a plot – they're just not interested. They don't remember we exist. And when they're *not* working it's worse! Moaning about lack of ideas. Mooching around the house all day. Getting under your feet and generally driving you crazy.'

Sheena laughed. 'I can well believe it. But I love Bruce, Mrs. Heathergill. Like you, I shan't mind.'

'That's our weakness, isn't it?' Janet's voice became unexpectedly tense. 'Here we are, cleaning spoons and

164

worrying ourselves sick. But are they worrying about us being worried? Not on your life! They're down there at the burnside, all eyes and ears and excitement – waiting for the showdown. They couldn't care less about our feelings!'

That Janet, usually so poised and calm, should talk in this way, betraying sharp anxiety behind the flippancy of her words, was a surprise for Sheena. Some of the anxiety transferred itself to her own mind, which had hitherto been basking comfortably in the warmth of her nearness to Bruce.

She stopped applying Silvaclean and said, 'D'you think Inspector MacLeod is going to make an arrest?'

'Why else did he arrange for them all to meet?' Janet put the back of one hand to her forehead, and for once her lips trembled. 'Oh, Sheena,' she said, 'I do hate the thought of – of violence! Violence that has been done. Violence that is going to be done. . . .'

Sheena could scarcely believe it – that the woman she admired more than anyone else in Breckadale should now be seeking help and comfort from her. Impulsively, she went across and knelt at Janet's feet. 'Don't be upset, Mrs. Heathergill. At least we're not concerned, personally.'

'Are you sure?'

'Well, I suppose we are – in the sense that everybody in the world must share the blame for violence. What I mean is, our menfolk are not directly involved. Bruce wouldn't hurt a mouse. As for Mr. Heathergill . . .'

'All right, dear.' Janet bent down and kissed her. 'We'll go on cleaning the spoons. It won't be long now before we know the truth.'

'No, it won't be long now,' said Sheena.

(5)

At this middle part of the day – and on account of the deteriorating weather – the golf course was empty, as MacLeod had guessed it would be. They were alone at McDermott's death-place.

They gathered on the sandy shingle beneath the turf bank – the inspector himself, carrying a golf club he had brought with him in the car; Sergeant MacPherson, inwardly nervous and excited but trying hard to reflect his superior's outward show of professional detachment; a young constable with a boyish face whose name, it appeared, was Smith; Hamish, tense and pale, his anxious eyes continually on the inspector's face; Bruce, dour and silent, hands in pockets, shoulders hunched; and Peter Marlin wearing a dark funeral suit and a snap-brim hat only a shade greyer than his face. The burn ran lapping past their feet, dark brown under the lowering sky.

Down at the river-mouth white spray was leaping where the incoming tide met the outflow of the Con. In an hour, as the salt water swelled into the fresh, the shingle would be completely covered; but by then the show would be over.

The knoll which overlooked the seventeenth green on the opposite bank sheltered MacLeod and the others

166

from the southerly wind, but they could hear it whining over above their heads. At times a downward eddy flung spits of rain in their faces. Across the bridge, Duncraig soared up from the dunes, grim and even sinister in the grey light. By all the signs, the afternoon was going to be wet and stormy, and already the caravanners were busy with ropes and tarpaulins, preparing for the worst.

Fingal's smiths were wielding their hammers with increasing violence.

A car came bucketing down the golf course track and drew up near the seventeenth green. Out of it stepped Colin Campbell, hatless and with a strip of sticking-plaster above his left eye. As he crossed the bridge and the loose boards rattled, a black arm-band was conspicuous against the light coloured material of his raincoat.

He joined them, exchanging a non-committal smile with Marlin. His words, however, were for the inspector.

'Well, is this a reconstruction of the crime?'

'Not exactly, Mr. Campbell.'

'Anyway, I'm glad you phoned and asked me to come. Waiting for the funeral was getting on my nerves.' He looked round and nodded to the others. 'Quite a parade for Finlay!' he said.

Impatiently, Bruce shifted his feet in the damp shingle. 'Tell me, Inspector – when does the curtain go up?'

'Right now, Mr. Cattanach.'

MacLeod rested the blade of the club against a small boulder and leant lightly on the grip, and Hamish noticed for the first time that it was a 9-iron, made for a left-hander.

Almost casually, the inspector went on, 'I have brought you here to the scene of the murder, gentlemen, because very soon I want to ask one of you a question – in the presence of another. What's more, you have all been under suspicion for the past two days, and you have a right to know how we eventually solved the problem of the murderer's identity.'

'Finlay would have appreciated this!' remarked Colin, his square chin jutting.

On the whole he appeared to be enjoying the situation. Hamish, on the other hand, his nerves strung taut, was beginning to loathe it. He had also a curious premonition of danger.

'It was evident from the beginning,' said MacLeod, 'that McDermott wasn't killed in the course of ordinary robbery. In his pockets were found a valuable cigarette-case and several pound notes. The motive, therefore, must have been a personal one.'

Astonished by his own temerity, Hamish blurted out, 'That was obvious even to me.'

'Quite so.' The inspector coughed. After a momentary pause, he continued, 'For instance, Mr. Cattanach here had a personal motive because of McDermott's attitude to Miss McRae.'

'I may have had a motive, but I'm damned if—'

'Take it easy, Mr. Cattanach. Mr. Campbell had one, too, because he inherits a considerable part of his cousin's estate.'

168

Colin frowned. 'That's true, in a way. At the same time, it was only afterwards—'

'So had Mr. Marlin. He wanted to marry Mc-Dermott's wife – who, however, had religious objections to divorce.'

'Look here, Inspector' – the big man moved forward, his shoes crunching in the shingle – 'd'you mind keeping Alice's name out of this! She knew nothing—'

'I'm sorry. I meant no offence to Mrs. McDermott.'

The apology was also a warning. Against the lap of the burn and the distant hammering in the cave, the cry of a peewit sounded melancholy and forlorn. Hamish had a longing to be back with Janet, safe and comfortable by the fireside.

'The process of murder,' MacLeod said, 'was uncomplicated. McDermott was tripped and knocked down and as he fell his attacker straddled him – like this, one foot on either side of the body – and struck at his head with some kind of club. McDermott was lying on his back, and the injuries were on the left side of his face. The club, therefore, must have been swung by a right-handed person.'

Hamish drew in his breath and stared at the inspector. He struggled to readjust the picture in his mind, as in a moment of sharp dismay, he realized that all along he had been looking at it in a mirror.

MacLeod said, 'Mr. Marlin being left-handed, that seemed to let him out.'

For once the big man's face lost its impassivity as he exclaimed, 'Seemed, Inspector?'

'Ay. And the fact that the injuries, according to the doctor, were caused by something made of metal rather than wood seemed to let Mr. Cattanach out, even though he is – or was – a shinty player.'

'I thought my camans would come into it!' said Bruce, tautly.

'In addition, Miss McRae provided Mr. Cattanach with an alibi by testifying that at the time of the murder they were together on the beach. Mr. Marlin had an alibi, too, because at nine minutes to eleven he was in the Breckadale Arms to receive a telephone call from Mr. Campbell.'

'Which also provides my alibi,' said Colin. 'I phoned from a box eight miles away.'

'Exactly,' replied MacLeod.

The blood pounded through Hamish's head, in time with the beat of the hammers. 'But Duncan,' he exclaimed, 'all this means that—'

'Please! Let me do it my way.'

Hamish fell silent, glancing round with a feeling almost of horror. It was evident now that Duncan possessed an ace that he himself had completely overlooked. It was evident now that he had been stupid to imagine that any amateur, however gifted in the art of writing, could pit his wits against a professional detective.

Marlin said quietly, 'I think I'm beginning to see it.'

'At this point, and quite by accident,' MacLeod continued, 'I came upon important evidence. Old Peggy

McAllister talked about the sparks from Fingal's anvil – the sparks that flew up against the sky.'

Hamish experienced the muscle-tightening cold of a man with a fever. The lapping burn, the waving red flag on the seventeenth green, the spray flying at the river-mouth – they all began to spin round in his brain. He closed his eyes in an effort to preserve both physical and mental balance.

Bruce started to say something, but the Inspector cut him short. 'As I thought of these sparks, it suddenly occurred to me that an alibi could have been faked. Yesterday evening, Mr. Marlin, while you and Mr. Campbell were at dinner, I took this 9-iron from your golf bag and told Sergeant MacPherson to have it examined in the laboratory in Kinloch.'

'So that's where it went!'

'Ay. This morning I learnt that traces of human blood had been found in the blade-grooves – blood of the same type as McDermott's.'

'But on Saturday night,' said Marlin, 'Colin had borrowed it.'

'I know. Mr. Campbell had also borrowed a portable telephone – a simple matter for a Post Office engineer, especially as it was one that had been put aside for repair. This instrument has two defects – Sergeant MacPherson found it yesterday in the store at Kinloch post office and today brought me a report on it. The webbing support-strap is missing. It was torn off on Saturday night, probably inadvertently, as Mr. Campbell was taking the instrument from the boot of his car.

171

Hurriedly he threw it away – into the burn. The tide carried it round to Fingal's Cave, and there, yesterday morning, old Dan Morrison fished it out of the water. There is also a fault in the wiring of the instrument. On Saturday night, when Mr. Campbell stood on the bonnet of his car and clipped it to the low wires in front of the green yonder, a shower of sparks flew up. He phoned Mr. Marlin all right – not from a call-box outside Kinloch but from the scene of the murder.'

Hamish opened his eyes. Through a bewildered haze he saw Colin's face, twisted in surprise. He saw Sergeant MacPherson and Constable Smith moving in behind him.

He heard Colin's angry voice, 'You're lying Inspector! I did phone from near Kinloch—'

'You told me yourself that by losing the match you were left with only half-a-crown. Half-a-crown is useless in a call-box.'

'I had some other change. I forgot—'

'Now, my question,' said MacLeod inexorably.

'You led Mr. Marlin and others to believe that your cousin's legacy came as a surprise. But on Friday night in the cocktail bar, Miss McRae overheard McDermott telling you in confidence that he'd changed his will in your favour. She remembered about it less than an hour ago. Wasn't it because of this – because you suddenly realized that she alone could definitely establish the motive that had led you to murder – wasn't it because of this that in a panic you tried to kill her – with one of your own golf clubs? And when you failed, didn't you then stage the "accident" to yourself, in order to divert suspicion?'

For Hamish the whole thing was an ugly dream, causing him to lose for a time the power of coherent action. Even when Colin suddenly leapt forward and struck the inspector in the face, he stood stock still, shaken by the violence that began to erupt around him. The violence of Colin as he snatched the club from MacLeod's hand and swung it viciously, clearing a path for himself. The violence of Bruce and young Smith as they dived forward only to be butted and kicked aside. The violence of the inspector's shout, 'Stop him, MacPherson!'

Gallantly, the sergeant plunged in, but the club whirled and thudded against his chest. As he doubled up and sank to his knees, gasping, Colin ran past him for the bridge, his blond hair flying in the wind.

Wiping blood from his chin, MacLeod went after him. So did Marlin. So did Bruce and Smith, who weren't badly hurt.

Pulling himself together, Hamish helped the sergeant to his feet. 'Come on, MacPherson. Can you make it?'

'Right, sir. I – I was only winded.'

They followed the others, some twenty yards in the rear, clattering over the bridge and turning in the direction of the dunes and Duncraig.

How Colin meant to escape – or even if he meant to escape at all – was never established. His pursuers were so close that he had no time to get into his own car and drive away, but he may have hoped to out-distance them and make use of one of the cars in the caravan park. Indeed, he did bear right to begin with, as if that were his intention.

Almost at once, however, he must have realized that those behind were in position to cut him off, and he swerved left again towards the Rock, his feet pounding violently in the soft sand of the dunes. He was fit and powerful, and it soon became apparent, as MacLeod and Marlin dropped back, that only Bruce and Smith would be able to keep pace with him.

MacPherson, throwing off the effects of his hurt, left Hamish behind and began to overhaul the others. By the time Colin had passed the old lifeboat house at the foot of Duncraig he was at the heels of MacLeod and Marlin.

Spray was whipping around the Rock, and the rain had come in earnest.

Panting as he climbed the steep folds of rock and turf, Hamish was conscious of his trouser-legs flapping wetly about his ankles. His angry hatred of the murderer had become tinged with pity. As one of the hunters, he himself felt sick and horrified. As the hunted, with knowledge of a mortal sin capping his terror, how did Colin feel?

Colin reached the summit, a platform of wind-blown turf scarcely twenty feet across.

On the outer edge, with the turbulent, white-capped water crawling far below, he turned to face his enemies, seeming only then to understand that he had run himself into an airy trap and that all his lung-bursting effort had been useless. His mouth sagged open in his struggle for breath. His face was twisted in mental pain. His sportsman's clear blue eyes were enlarged like an animal's. But he stood his ground, taking a fresh grip of the club as if ready to fight.

Hamish scrambled up the last few slippery feet. He hated heights, and Duncraig always made him dizzy. Today he felt as insecure as a tight-rope walker. The bitter rain struck his face. He looked beyond Colin and saw the hazy grey backdrop of Sanda, Ailsa Craig and the rolling hills of Ayrshire.

MacLeod and MacPherson began to move in on their quarry, while Marlin, Bruce and Smith manoeuvred warily to get behind him. To Hamish the picture was evil – the slow beginning to yet another death. Often he had described similar scenes in fiction, but only now did he fully comprehend the tragic sickness of humanity that caused them.

'Don't move, Campbell!' MacLeod's voice was thin against the elemental sounds of wind and sea. 'Be sensible. . . .'

'You can't do this to me!' wailed Colin, his despair so uncharacteristic of the once gay and brash young golfer that it made Hamish flinch. 'You can't do it, Inspector! I was in debt. Those bookies—'

'I know. I've seen their accounts.' MacLeod was within two yards of him now. 'Colin Finlay Campbell,' he began, still carrying out his duty, 'you are charged with the murder of your cousin, Finlay McDermott. Anything you say may be—'

Colin may have lost his footing. Hamish was never sure. But suddenly he was staggering on the edge of the precipice, his shoes rasping on the meagre grass, the club flung high.

Smith sprang in from the side to catch him. And he would have caught him had not Bruce – apparently by accident – stumbled against Smith and knocked him sprawling. Next moment Colin was gone, shrieking as he plummeted down.

Hamish saw Bruce, on his knees, looking in his direction. Death had come horribly to a human being, but it had come swiftly – and perhaps by his own will. In a small, clear moment of time he knew that Bruce's clumsy movement had been no accident but an impulsive gesture in support of man's freedom to control his destiny.

Slowly, and with pain in his heart, he nodded approval.

The thudding sound still came up from Fingal's Cave, like hammers on an anvil.